MURDER AT THE [illegible]

I walked briskly back to Redwood Cove Be [illegible] Helen was starting to put out the appetizers in the parlor. I joined her with a tray of wineglasses, then retrieved a bottle of chardonnay from the refrigerator and a merlot from the wine rack. I opened them and put the bottles next to the glasses.

I returned to my rooms, did some more paperwork, and was starting to think about dinner when my cell phone rang.

"Hello?"

"Kelly, I need your help."

I knew it was Rudy's voice, but there was a quavering quality to it I'd never heard before.

"Rudy, what's happened?"

"The police found a body on the *Nadia*."

"What! Who?"

"Alexander Koskov. He was shot..."

Books by Janet Finsilver

MURDER AT REDWOOD COVE

MURDER AT THE MANSION

MURDER AT THE FORTUNE TELLER'S TABLE

MURDER AT THE MUSHROOM FESTIVAL

MURDER AT THE MARINA

Published by Kensington Publishing Corporation

Murder at the Marina

Janet Finsilver

LYRICAL UNDERGROUND
Kensington Publishing Corp.
www.kensingtonbooks.com

LYRICAL UNDERGROUND BOOKS are published by

Kensington Publishing Corp.
119 West 40th Street
New York, NY 10018

First Electronic Edition: April 2019
ISBN-13: 978-1-5161-0424-6 (ebook)
ISBN-10: 1-5161-0424-2 (ebook)

First Print Edition: April 2019
ISBN-13: 978-1-5161-0425-3
ISBN-10: 1-5161-0425-0

Printed in the United States of America

To E.J., my husband, who is always there for me.

Acknowledgments

My husband, E.J., accompanies me on my journeys to fictitious Redwood Cove. He's always willing and ready to help with questions I have or to give me feedback, which I greatly appreciate. My amazing writing group made up of Colleen Casey, Staci McLaughlin, Ann Parker, Carole Price, and Penny Warner gave me phenomenal comments about my chapters, as well as many opportunities to share laughter. My two beta readers, Cyndie Bell and Linda Uhrenholt, provided very useful feedback with their thoughtful reading of this book. My friend Monique Young was a tremendous resource when it came to Russian history. I am very lucky to work with an outstanding agent, Dawn Dowdle, and a great editor, John Scognamiglio. They both give me a great deal of support. Thank you all!

Chapter 1

My heart raced as the Appaloosa galloped down the beach, his hooves flinging sand high into the air. I balanced my weight in the saddle and urged him on. The horse lengthened his stride, stretching his body full out, his gait long and smooth. It was the first time I'd let him run so fast. I knew the packed sand along the water's edge would absorb the shock of the hard run and protect his legs.

Crashing waves spewed foam on my right as they encountered rocky outcroppings jutting up from the Pacific Ocean. The tang of the salt air filled my lungs. An occasional spray of water landed on Nezi and me. My eyes teared as the wind whipped past.

I didn't want it to end, but he'd run long enough. I began pulling him in. Nezi pulled back at the bit, apparently not wanting it to end either. I continued the gentle, firm pressure on the reins. Slowly, he responded. His pace became a gentle canter, then a trot, and finally an energetic walk. Water lapped around his feet as a dying wave reached us.

I'd had many great rides on my family's Wyoming ranch, but none of them had filled my senses like what I'd just experienced. The bright blue ocean, the black rocks, and the slate gray cliffs towering high on my left, alternated with the dense green redwood forest of Northern California. Narrow ribbons of runoff water meandered their way to the ocean across the sand. The smells and sounds of the sea mixed together—an orchestra of sensation. Ocean mist covered my face and my skin tingled from its cool touch. Adrenaline coursed through my body after the exhilarating ride.

I took a deep breath and headed toward a path winding up and away from the beach. The salty ocean air became fainter as it mingled with the earthy scents of the redwood forest. Sunlight dappled the trail and leaves muted Nezi's hoofbeats. A stream ran near the trail, and I reined Nezi over to it to give him a drink. I stopped in a bright patch of sunlight. As the horse lowered his head, I leaned back in the saddle and soaked up the rays.

He plunged his nose in and took long sips. Suddenly, he began pawing at the water.

"You go ahead and have fun, boy. You deserve it. That was a wonderful ride." I patted his slim neck with its white background covered by assorted black spots ranging in size from a dime to a half dollar.

Liquid diamonds flew into the air and cascaded down as he splashed. True horseplay! Nezi shook his head, snorted, and turned his head to look at me. A white crescent moon framed his dark brown eye.

I looked at my watch. "Time to head back," I told him.

We got back on the trail and headed for Redwood Cove Stable. We emerged from the forest, and the barn and the white-fenced paddocks with lush green grass were straight ahead. I stopped at a hitching rail, dismounted, and tied Nezi to it. He had lathered up during the run, but the walk had dried him off.

I removed the saddle and pad I had brought from home when Diane Wilcox, the owner of the stable, had offered to let me ride Nezi when he was available. She had given me a place to stow my gear, which I really appreciated. I headed for the tack room. I took Nezi's halter off a peg with his name under it and put my saddle on the stand I'd been given to use.

I opened the refrigerator in the tack room and took out the container of carrot chunks I'd brought as a treat for Nezi. I chose a brush from the ones lined up on a shelf next to the door. The sweet scent of alfalfa enveloped me as I passed several light green bales of hay.

Returning to Nezi, I replaced his bridle with the halter and tied him to the post with a rope. I placed a piece of carrot on my outstretched palm and offered it to the Appaloosa. He grabbed it and munched as I brushed. Several pieces of carrot later and he was ready to go into his stall. I led him to it and offered him my shoulder as a rubbing post, a way of saying thank you. I gave him a last pat, stopped at the tack room to put his bridle away, and left.

When I emerged from the barn, I found Diane standing at the hitching rail talking to a middle-aged man. The word *long* came to mind as I looked at him. He was tall, probably about six feet four, with arms dangling down his sides and Abraham Lincoln legs. Soft brown curls covered his head.

Diane smiled at me. "Hi, Kelly. How was the ride?"

"Fantastic! Thank you so much for letting me take Nezi out."

"Happy to do it. It's good for him to get the exercise." She turned to the gentleman next to her. "I'd like you to meet Tom Brodsky. Tom, this is Kelly Jackson, manager of Redwood Cove Bed and Breakfast."

He thrust out his hand. "Nice to meet you."

"Likewise," I said, and we shook.

Diane looked at the clipboard in her hand. "Tom is involved in planning for the Russian Heritage Festival that's taking place next weekend. We were finalizing plans for a Cossack riding team to stable their horses here during the event."

"Their horsemanship skills are legendary." I looked at Tom. "Will they be performing for the public?"

"Yes. The festival schedule is online, if you're interested."

"I'll definitely make it a point to come to see them," I said.

"The entire event is a lot of fun," Tom said. "Our goals are to teach people about our Russian heritage, as well as raise funds for educational scholarships. We'll have everything from rope making to basket weaving to candle rolling. It's all interactive. There are a multitude of singing and dancing groups as well."

"I'll look it up when I get back to the inn."

"I understand there's a new location this year," Diane said. "I heard it'll be held outside of Redwood Cove instead of at Fort Nelsen."

A frown creased Tom's forehead. "Yeah. Not my idea." He sighed. "It is what it is."

Diane lowered her clipboard. "Everything looks complete in terms of the horses. We'll have everything ready when the Cossacks arrive, and I'll have the house trailer at the event field tomorrow."

"Thanks, Diane." He turned to me. "One of the organizers from San Francisco is bringing a setup crew and asked me to find accommodations for them. Diane kindly offered to let us use her trailer."

"That sounds like a good plan. They'll be on site," I said.

Diane smiled at Tom. "He's part of the Russian Heritage committee. I was happy to be able to help."

Tom looked at me. "I'll be at your inn tomorrow for a committee meeting."

"I saw it listed on the calendar."

"I'd better be going," Tom said. "Nice to meet you, Ms. Jackson."

"Please call me Kelly. I'll see you tomorrow."

Tom walked off toward the parking lot.

Diane turned to me. "Glad you had fun, Kelly. I'm looking forward to when we can get in a ride together."

"Me, too." We said our good-byes, and I headed for my Jeep.

I was going to meet Rudy and Ivan Doblinsky, two Russian brothers I'd met when I arrived in Redwood Cove. I had encountered them my first day at the inn, when Ivan's roar of, "It's murder and you know it" had made its way down the hall of Redwood Cove Bed and Breakfast and into my living quarters. That hadn't boded well for the first day of my new job, and I had headed out to find the source. That's when I met the Silver Sentinels, a crime-solving group of senior citizens, of which Rudy and Ivan were members.

That was months ago. Today, I was on my way to see their fishing boat, *Nadia*. She'd come up in conversation a number of times, and I was looking forward to seeing her. I drove up the road toward the marina, located north of the town of Fort Peter.

On my way there, I decided to take a short detour to see the bed and breakfast my boss, Michael Corrigan, had just purchased. He owned the company I worked for, called Resorts International, and was passionate about restoring historic properties.

I stopped in front of a lovely but faded three-story colonial-style home. Curlicues of gingerbread trim adorned the eaves, their paint peeling but still in place. It would be fun to come back after the restoration to see the grand lady as she once looked.

I continued on to the marina, found a parking space, and changed my cowboy boots for tennis shoes. I looked at my watch and saw I was early but decided to see if the brothers had already arrived. They had given me directions, but what was crystal clear to them had me a little confused. I walked in the general direction of where I thought I was supposed to go, aware of the slight smell of fish.

I spied a man in baggy denim bib overalls wearing a dusty black Giants baseball cap, his gray hair curled up over its sides. He basked in the sun outside a small bait shop in a rocking chair. Fishing nets and tackle equipment hung on the building's gray boards. Handwritten signs advertising LIVE SARDINES AND BAIT SHRIMP were tacked on the wall. An old, personalized fluorescent clock declared it to be TIM'S PLACE.

I approached him. "Hi, I'm Kelly Jackson." I smiled. "Are you Tim?"

"Nope. He ain't here no more. Done moved on. I'm Joe." The missing front tooth didn't mar the congeniality in his voice.

"I'm here to meet the Doblinsky brothers at their boat, *Nadia*. I'm wondering if you could help me with directions."

"Sure. Glad to." He pointed an arthritic finger in the direction of a gate. "Walk on through there. It ain't locked right now. The boat's down apiece on the left."

A few minutes later, I stood in front of a large white vessel with black trim. *Nadia* in large bold black letters on the bow assured me I'd found what I'd been seeking.

"Rudy…Ivan…are you here?" I called out.

I didn't get a response and decided to knock on the cabin door. I grabbed the metal rails next to an opening and boarded the boat. My knock brought no response. I could clearly see into the galley below. A tidy compact kitchen, a boothed dining area, and a small table filled the area. A living room with built-in couches along both sides of the wall occupied the right side.

The dining table was in clear view, with a shaft of sunlight illuminating it. I caught a glimpse of a multicolored object sparkling in the sun's bright light at the table's edge. I stepped a little to the side and craned my neck to see better.

What I saw was the hilt of a dagger.

The handle glinted in the sun, but the curved blade didn't shine like the rest of it.

A dull, rust-colored material covered the metal…the color of dried blood.

The cold hand of fear squeezed my heart.

Chapter 2

My breath quickened. I stepped back and grabbed my cell phone from my pocket. Was what I saw enough to call 911? I could try to reach Deputy Stanton directly. I'd met him, along with Rudy and Ivan, on my first day. The No Cell Phone Service signal brought an answer to my dilemma. I'd have to find a pay phone.

I turned to go, then stopped. What if that *was* blood on the knife? Someone might be hurt. I had to search the boat to be sure no one was inside injured.

The brothers had told me where a key to the cabin door was located, in case they were late. They had sheepishly admitted they often forgot to bring their key, so they kept a spare on the boat. I went to the equipment box mounted against the cabin a few feet from the door and opened it. It was filled with frayed netting. Three rusty boxes were stacked on top of each other in a back corner. The key was in the bottom one.

I unlocked the cabin door, then hesitated. If there was an attacker on board, I needed to be prepared to defend myself. I scanned the deck but saw nothing useful. I took a deep breath, opened the door, and peered in. A wooden ladder led down to the living area. Equipment hung on the wall at the bottom next to the dining area. No one was under the ladder.

I descended the stairs and stopped to listen. The only sound was the gentle lapping of the ever-moving ocean on the sides of the boat...and the pounding of my heart. I didn't call out again. If someone wanted me to know they were there, they would've answered my knock.

I surveyed the objects on the wall. There was a sturdy-looking pole with a hooked end I could use. I took it off its peg and gripped it tightly.

I stood next to the galley, and a quick look around revealed no signs of a struggle or blood. I glanced at the knife. Gemstones of many sizes and colors along the hilt sparkled in the sun's bright light. The curved metal blade could do some serious damage and maybe had, considering the color of the substance on it.

I walked across the living area to a place concealed by curtains, raised the pole, and held it tightly. I prepared to pull back the covering that blocked off the bow. I'd been on some fishing trips with my family and had some knowledge of the layout of boats. I suspected this was a sleeping area. Holding my breath, I pulled the curtain aside. I exhaled with a whoosh when I found a neatly made bed covered with an open navy blue sleeping bag and clearly no body-size lumps under it.

Going to the stern, I discovered two small rooms empty of people but full of gear. No one lurked in the bathroom. I climbed up the ladder and went outside, thankful to be out of the cramped quarters. I wanted to check the deck for anywhere an injured person might be. I looked out at the water and saw two small motorboats nearby. Each had a fisherman in it. They were close enough to hear me if I screamed for help.

I gripped my weapon and went around the boat, checking under tarpaulins and behind anything big enough to conceal a person. Several large "person-size" bins were empty. Time to call Stanton. I locked the cabin and headed for the bait shop to find a phone I could use.

As I got close to the shop, a deputy sheriff's car drove in. I wouldn't be needing a phone after all. Gus, the police bloodhound Deputy Stanton was minding for a fellow officer on vacation, stuck his large head and droopy ears out the back window. The driver's door opened and the impressively broad shoulders of Deputy Bill Stanton appeared. He got out and headed in my direction.

I waved and said, "Hi…Bill."

It was still difficult for me to call him by his first name. Our first few months of getting to know each other had involved crimes I helped solve, along with the Silver Sentinels. We had kept our relationship formal. When Redwood Cove was running smoothly, we'd decided to go to a first-name basis now that I was a town resident.

I wondered if we'd be back to formal in the not-too-distant future. A knife with what appeared to be blood on it had been found on Rudy and Ivan's boat. They were friends and members of the Silver Sentinels. Was I about to get involved in another investigation? Time would tell.

"Kelly, I didn't expect to see you here," he said.

"I'm meeting Rudy and Ivan to see their boat. I just checked and they aren't here yet."

I filled him in on what I'd seen and done as we walked to the boat together.

Stanton nodded. "We got an anonymous phone call about a bloody dagger being seen on a boat called *Nadia*. The caller made it clear it wasn't any piece of fishing equipment or someone's steak knife. That's what brought me out here."

I waited on the deck while Stanton searched the boat. Curious, I went to the window where I'd first seen the weapon. I definitely had to crane my neck to see it, as it was almost directly beneath me on the table. I looked through the window next to it, but a lamp blocked my view. A person could see it more easily from the opposite side, but that would mean they had been walking around the boat. The dagger couldn't be spotted by a casual glance. I wondered who had placed the call.

Stanton came to the door and waved me in. "I didn't see any sign of a struggle."

"I didn't either."

We were quiet for a moment, staring at the object on the table. I leaned closer to get a better look. The gold metal on the hilt had intricate designs around each gem. An artist had etched a scene with several horsemen astride their mounts running down the side. The attention to detail was such, I could see the muscles of the horses.

I had a feeling the jewels we were looking at were real.

Three emeralds, each larger than a nickel, lined the top of the handle. Diamonds surrounded each stone. The horses ran along a ruby road. The part of the curved blade I could see had what appeared to be the work of the same artist depicting a battle scene.

I straightened my back. "Not any ordinary knife."

"I agree. If those are real jewels, it's worth a fortune."

"Bill, while I was waiting for you on the deck, I thought about how someone would be able to see the knife. It wasn't easy from the window I used, and you can't see it from the window next to it because it's blocked. You could see it from the windows on the other side of the galley, but that would mean someone walked around the boat."

"Good thinking, Kelly. Our anonymous caller is a trespasser."

A tooting horn I'd become familiar with announced the arrival of the Redwood Cove/Fort Peter bus.

"I'm guessing Ivan and Rudy just arrived," I said.

We climbed the ladder and stood on the deck. The brothers were walking toward us. There was never a concern about confusing Rudy and Ivan, even at a distance. Ivan towered over his brother.

For every one of Ivan's rough edges, Rudy had a neat line.

Ivan's coarse gray hair had a life of its own. I'd seen him brush it, only to have it spring back up in every direction. Rudy's silver hair, on the other hand, had a soft sheen and seemed to be happy to stay in place, each hair having found a permanent home.

Ivan's mustache was a mate for his hair. He'd tried to train it once, only to declare defeat with loud grumbles. Rudy's didn't have a hair out of place, and military precision would describe the perfect line of his cut.

Ivan's loud voice boomed despite his efforts to control it, and his Russian accent was more pronounced than his brother's. Rudy was a quiet man and spoke almost perfect English unless he was flustered.

"Hi, Kelly. You beat us here." Ivan stood a little straighter and puffed out his chest. "What you think of our *Nadia*?"

"She's beautiful, Ivan." I looked at the dazzling white boat and the sparkling brass. "Your love for her shows with the great care you've given her."

"Yah. She's our *Nadia*." He beamed affectionately at the boat.

Rudy looked at Deputy Stanton quizzically. "Deputy Stanton, to what do we owe the pleasure of your visit?"

Stanton got right to the point. "Got a call about a dagger possibly covered in blood on a table on your boat."

"What?" Rudy's shocked tone matched the stunned look on Ivan's face.

The deputy inclined his head toward the boat's cabin. "Come see."

They climbed on the boat, then descended into the main quarters. Rudy walked to the table and stopped, his eyes glued to the jeweled weapon.

"Is that your knife?" Stanton asked.

"Uh…maybe."

"What do you mean, maybe?"

"I have one like it a home, or at least the last I knew, that's where it was. I haven't looked at it in a while."

"You have a knife just like this…jewels and all?" Stanton asked.

Rudy nodded. "Yes. So…that one's mine…or one identical to it."

Chapter 3

"Do you know what's on the blade?" Deputy Stanton asked.

"No idea," Rudy replied.

"Okay. I want all of you to wait outside. I'm going to take another look around."

We waited in silence on the dock. It was quiet except for the water softly slapping the boat and the occasional raucous cry of a seagull searching for a bite to eat. Rudy began pacing, his hands held tightly behind his back, his mouth turned downward.

Deputy Stanton eventually joined us, holding the knife in an evidence bag. "I'd like you to stay off the boat until we know more about what's on the knife."

The brothers nodded in agreement.

"I'm going to drop this off at the lab. Then, Rudy, I'd like to come by to see if you still have your dagger."

"I understand. I'll look for it as soon as I get home."

The deputy left.

"I'm sorry there'll be no tour of the boat today, Kelly," Rudy said.

"Another time." I shared with them that I'd had a quick look around when I searched the boat. "Let me give you both a ride home."

"Thank you. We appreciate." Ivan's usually loud voice was more of a mumble.

It was a silent ride, except for Rudy's directions to their home in Redwood Cove. I turned a corner, and Ivan pointed to a house with a giant anchor embedded in the front yard. It was located on a knoll and faced the ocean with no other houses nearby. I pulled in the driveway and parked.

"Kelly, please come in," Rudy said. "Have some tea."

"I don't want to intrude," I responded.

"No, please." His voice had a desperate note. "I am nervous. Haven't had interaction with police before. Bad that dagger is on *Nadia*."

Stress had his usually perfect English slipping away.

"Of course I'll stay if you feel I can help in any way."

His face relaxed. "Thank you so much."

We walked up a path of gray stepping stones to the front door. The yard was filled with native grasses I'd seen growing on the headlands. The house's light gray exterior blended with the silver strands of the vegetation. A carved ship graced the wooden front door Rudy opened.

We entered a living room with large plate-glass windows framing the Pacific Ocean. A navy blue couch had two blue plaid armchairs on either side of it. I glimpsed a chess set on a coffee table as we made our way to the kitchen.

The sink was off to one side. Cabinets lined the wall to the left of it, and the counter stretched to the right, with windows running its full length. The bright blue of the sea filled the view. The windows continued on to a dining area with a table and four chairs.

"Stunning vista of the ocean," I said.

"This was our uncle's house," Ivan said. "He raise us. The sea has always been part of our lives, and he want it to be with us for as long as we lived."

"I'll go see if I still have my dagger," Rudy said. "Kelly, please have a seat at the table."

Ivan reached for a metal teakettle. "I make drink."

I pulled out one of the sturdy wooden chairs and settled on the soft cushion covering the seat.

Ivan brought over a tin of different types of tea. "We have choices."

The whistle of the teakettle announced the water was ready. Ivan brought me a mug, and I chose a lemon-flavored tea. He poured in the water, and I held the mug while the tea steeped, enjoying the warmth. The sweet scent was soothing after the tense afternoon.

Ivan put a blue-and-white container of shortbread cookies on the table, then joined me and chose a cinnamon tea. The scents mingled together, creating a wholesome spiciness in the air.

Rudy returned, holding a silver case in his hands. "I still have my dagger."

He placed the box on the table. The cover had the same ornate engraving I'd seen on the knife but no jewels.

"This is the traveling container for the daggers."

Daggers? Rudy knew there was more than one of these knives that were works of art?

He opened the box, revealing a knife in a sheath with two empty slots next to it that had the names *Verushka* and *Timur* on metal plates. The dagger in the case had the name *Rudolf* above it. The sheath covering the blade matched the handle in its ornateness and its jewels.

"Verushka and Timur are my half sister and half brother. I haven't seen them since I was a child. The daggers and the case were to be given to us by our father when we came of age. He was a member of an aristocratic Russian family."

An aristocratic Russian family? The only thing I knew about their background was that they were fishermen. The surprises kept coming.

He took his knife out of its sheath and pointed to the battle scene on the blade. "This tells a tale of victory and was meant to bring good luck."

A knock on the door interrupted us. Rudy put down his knife on the table, left, and returned with Deputy Sheriff Stanton.

"There's my knife." Rudy pointed at the table.

Stanton examined the case and Rudy gave him the same explanation I'd just heard.

"So, it would seem the knife on the boat belongs to one of them. Do you know how to get in touch with them?"

Rudy shook his head. "We left Russia as children." His shoulders sagged. "I will tell you our story. First, Deputy Stanton, would you like some tea?"

"No, thanks. Appreciate you asking."

Rudy and Stanton pulled out chairs and sat. Rudy then shared the story of his and Ivan's lives. Their mother, Tatiana, worked as a maid for a Russian aristocratic family. Her husband, Ivan's father, was lost at sea about the same time Prince Zharkov lost his wife during the birth of their third child. Ivan was three at the time.

Rudy spread his hands and shrugged. "They were both young and grieving…and drawn to each other. Then I came along."

Rudy explained the prince wanted to marry Tatiana, but the family forbade it. If he'd gone against their wishes, he would've had to give up his title and inheritance, creating a hardship for his children. He chafed at the position he was in, but at least he and Tatiana could be together.

"Political unrest was common in Russia," Rudy said. "The family lived in a very remote part of the country, and they hoped it wouldn't reach them. They were fine for a very long time. However, in the late 1930s the situation became such the family knew it was time to flee."

It was decided the family would split up so they could move faster and be less conspicuous. Ivan and Rudy went with one of the family's uncles, while their mother went with the prince to help him care for his other children, one of whom was very sickly. The prince's parents and a couple of staff members formed a third group. America was their goal, and they planned to meet again in San Francisco.

"Most of what the family decided to take, including the dagger case, came with us," Rudy said. "Two boys and a man with a wagon could move faster and had more room to pack items. We didn't need much space for our personal needs," Rudy said.

Ivan nodded. "We travel for many days."

Unfortunately, the reunion never took place. Rudy, Ivan, and their uncle made it to San Francisco but found they were soon being pursued in that city. They changed their names and went into hiding. The uncle had fishing knowledge and enough funds to purchase a vessel. They lived on the sea and, along with a small crew, earned a living. Rudy explained he was a young boy at the time and his uncle told him all this when he was older. They didn't know if the others made it to the United States or not.

"When our uncle neared the end of his life, he gave me the knife and case. I didn't know about it until then." He caressed the empty slots. "I was close to Verushka and Timur. When you're part of an aristocratic family, there aren't a lot of children you're allowed to play with."

"Seems as if finding the knife could mean they made it," Stanton said.

"Possibly," Rudy replied. "Or it could've been stolen in Russia and come to this country with someone else."

"How on earth did it make it to Fort Peter and end up on your boat?" I asked.

The brothers shook their heads.

A valuable knife last seen in Russia crossed the sea to land on the Doblinsky brothers' fishing vessel...with a blade possibly covered in blood. This was a puzzle to rival any of the ones the Silver Sentinels and I had unraveled in the past.

Chapter 4

I took a sip of my tea and found it cold. I'd been so mesmerized by the tale of the family torn apart and their struggles, I'd forgotten all about my drink.

Deputy Stanton leaned back in his chair. "That's quite a story, Rudy. Thanks for sharing it."

Rudy looked at Ivan. "I wonder if Mother and the others made it after all."

Ivan went to the stove and started another kettle of water. "Yah. Maybe."

"We've searched for years," Rudy said. "When the Internet became a way of life, we thought maybe we'd find out what happened to them. But no luck."

Stanton stood. "I'll let you know if we discover anything about your family, and I'll call as soon as we have the lab report on the knife."

"Thanks, Deputy Stanton," Rudy said.

"My tea cold. So is yours, then," Ivan said to me.

The officer left, and I accepted the fresh mug of hot water Ivan offered me. The lemon tea had suited me both in fragrance and taste and I chose another bag of it.

Rudy gazed at the knife. "I remember the trek across Russia very well," he mused. "We disguised ourselves as peasants and walked beside our horse and wagon. It was a long, cold, tiring trip. Our uncle bought us passage on a large steamer to complete our journey. Before getting on the ship, we shed our work clothes and became part of a businessman's family. The prince's money assured us decent quarters. We were better off than many. The trip was difficult."

Ivan put his hands around his mug. "Yah. Very long time on ship. San Francisco. So happy to see it. Beautiful."

Rudy smiled. "That's a day I remember well. Putting my feet on the ground again, though it took a while before it felt like the earth wasn't constantly moving under me."

Ivan laughed. "Yah. We held on to each other, but not help much."

Rudy closed the case that held the dagger. "We spent a couple of weeks in a hotel. My uncle made friends with people in the Russian community. Then he began to hear rumors that people knew we were part of an aristocratic family. Threats followed. We went into hiding and then onto the fishing boat."

"Now we are here," Ivan said.

That summed it up.

"We have a few pictures. Would you like to see them, Kelly?"

"Absolutely."

"Let's go in the living room," Rudy said. "They are in there."

Ivan and I picked up our mugs and followed him. He stopped in front of shelves that lined one wall and pointed to a framed black-and-white photograph. "This is the only picture we have of the prince and my mother together."

A tall, dark-haired man resplendent in dress uniform stared into the camera. Ropes of braided material adorned the front of his military attire and his jacket had fringed shoulder epaulets. He wore knee-high leather boots. Next to him stood a pretty, petite woman wearing a long skirt and a puffy-sleeved striped blouse. Their mother's hair had been pulled up into a bun on top of her head. Her eyes glowed as she held the hand of her handsome prince. Smiles lit up their faces.

Rudy put the photo back on the shelf. "The prince loved our mother very much. He refused to let his family stop their relationship."

"You can see it in their faces," I said.

He pointed to the picture next to the one of his mother. "This is Timur and Verushka."

A young girl wearing a frilly white dress with long ringlets tied up in a big bow stood next to a boy wearing dark pants and a light-colored shirt. Her hand rested on his shoulder.

"The prince treated Ivan and me well. He made sure we both received schooling, though Ivan was placed with a different group of children belonging to the servants. I was allowed to be taught with the prince's other children by a private tutor."

Perhaps their education hadn't been quite equal, hence the differences in the way they spoke.

"The house had the classic onion domes of Russia and seemed to go on forever, room after room. The formal dining hall was so enormous, Timur, Verushka, and I would see if we could yell loud enough to get an echo."

He handed me a photo of himself and Ivan. "This is the last one we have."

Ivan had his arm around Rudy's shoulders, dwarfing him more than usual. I could see the resemblance in their childhood faces. Tents had been set up and white cloths had been put over tables. Horses and buggies appeared in the background.

"Fun picnics. I remember those," Ivan said.

Rudy sipped his tea. "A picnic with an aristocratic family was quite an event. Silver, cloth napkins, servants ever present."

"Lots of food in big baskets. Best part!" Ivan added.

I put the photo back on the shelf with the others. A Russian time now past.

Ivan sat on the couch and Rudy joined him. I settled in one of the armchairs. It felt good to sink into its softness.

Rudy frowned. "Kelly, what happens now? If that's blood on the knife, am I in trouble?"

"If the knife was used to commit a crime, the police would have to connect you to it for there to be a problem. That won't happen because you didn't do anything."

Rudy's face cleared. "You hear stories, you know. It's scary to have the dagger show up on our boat and be connected with our family."

"I understand." I put down my tea. "I'd better get going. Don't hesitate to call me if you have any questions or want to talk."

"Thanks, Kelly. It was nice to have you here."

We said our good-byes with assurances to schedule a boat tour when everything was back to normal.

As I drove up the driveway to Redwood Cove Bed and Breakfast, I looked in the rearview mirror and saw Tommy Rogers, the towheaded, ten-year-old son of the inn's assistant and baker, Helen, pedaling his bike hard. He leaned precariously from side to side. Tommy and his mother lived in a small cottage on the property.

I pulled into the parking lot in back, stopped, and put my arms on top of the steering wheel. I leaned forward and rested my chin on them, waiting to see the explosion of activity I knew was about to ensue.

Tommy skidded to a halt and leaned his bike against the porch. The back door flew open and a short-legged, tricolored basset hound flew out the door, ears flapping wildly. Tommy's laugh of sheer delight filled the air. Along with Fred's baying, they formed a harmonious duet. Their joy was a pleasure to see.

I loved my new life as manager of the inn. The white wooden building, with its gingerbread trim, had been built by the Anderson family, wealthy timber merchants, in the 1800s. A profusion of colorful flowers traveled up the side of a trellis. Their perfume would greet me as I walked to the house.

Helen opened the back door and gave me a wave. "Enough, you two. Tommy, come on in. I have a snack ready for you." Her hair, brown with a few gray streaks, had been clipped up at the back of her head.

I got out of the truck and followed the duo of Fred and Tommy into the inn. Helen had milk and cookies out on the granite counter on my right, which separated the kitchen from the main room. The large area was used as a gathering place and work area. Ahead of me, along the far wall, there were a couch, chairs, a woodburning stove, and a television. A large oak table on the left served for dining when we had big groups, and a surface to scatter folders when business called.

A sweet smell filled the air. Helen was carefully peeling thin sheets of dough from a stack and placing them on a baking tray. A jar of honey was next to it. The label proclaimed it to be organic. A bowl of chopped nuts rested next to the golden substance.

"What are you making?"

"Baklava for the Russian Heritage Committee that's meeting here tomorrow. The dessert was a special request from them."

"What goes in it?"

"There are layers of phyllo dough, nuts, butter, honey, sugar, and a few other ingredients. The phyllo is the challenge because it's so delicate."

Helen's baking skills were unlimited. I, on the other hand, didn't even want to stand next to the delicate-looking pastry. I'd probably make the sheets fuse together. Helen had free time in the afternoon and had started a baking business. Resorts International was happy to have her use the inn's kitchen. Often, what she was preparing was for our customers.

"How has your day been?" she asked.

"I had a wonderful ride on the beach, then met with Rudy and Ivan." I shared with her what had happened and what I had learned.

"That's quite a story. I wonder if they'll be able to find out how the knife got there."

"I do, too. I'm going to go freshen up, then I'll help get the wine and appetizers together for the guests."

"Everything is in the refrigerator, ready to go. I took care of it before I became stuck in honey and dough."

I walked down the hall and opened the door to my quarters. I, too, had a view that made the ocean part of my life and another reason I was thrilled to live here. Glass windows straight ahead of me framed the blue Pacific Ocean, a sandy beach, and rugged cliffs. On my right, the inn's garden and profuse multicolored flowers filled the scene.

I went into my kitchen, which was about the same size as the one on the *Nadia*. Compact, but it had everything I needed and one thing I didn't need but enjoyed—a commercial-size coffeemaker. My boss prized a good cup of coffee and made sure his employees had an opportunity to enjoy a savory brew as well.

I brushed my red hair, then found a sturdy clip to hold my now Brillo Pad locks under control. The ocean spritz during my horseback ride had created a mass of wiry, tight curls. I washed my hands and went back to the inn's kitchen.

Helen sprinkled chopped nuts on the now-full baking sheets. "Done, except for the cooking. I had enough ingredients to make two batches, so there'll be some for us as well."

I put out the evening refreshments for the guests, then went back to my rooms for my dinner of leftovers from a previous meal. I checked email as I ate, then returned to the parlor to clean up the area. The heavenly scent of Helen's baking made me hungry as I cleaned the dishes. I grabbed a chocolate chip cookie from the guest jar to keep my hunger demons at bay.

I noticed the knife rack as I left the kitchen. As I got ready to call it quits for the night, questions filled my mind. Why would someone leave an extremely valuable knife on the boat? And how did it involve Rudy and Ivan? Was it a threat or a warning because it appeared to be covered in blood?

Even worse, were the brothers in danger?

Chapter 5

The next morning passed quickly, between helping with the guests' breakfast baskets, paying bills, and ordering supplies. I closed the folder I'd been working on and rose to check the conference room. The Russian Heritage Committee was meeting at one o'clock, and I wanted to see if they had everything they needed. As I neared the room, I heard loud, boisterous voices, many with heavy Russian accents.

I paused at the entrance to the room and looked at the silver plaque over the door proclaiming it the SILVER SENTINELS' CONFERENCE ROOM. Michael Corrigan had had the idea after the crime-solving group of senior citizens had helped the community by being instrumental in catching a killer. Five members comprised the group. Besides Rudy and Ivan, there was the Professor, aka Herbert Winthrop, a retired Berkeley professor, Mary Rutledge, and Gertrude Plumber, Gertie as she liked to be called.

I entered the room and made my way between the groups of people engaged in animated conversation. Teacups abounded, and I saw Helen was on top of things as usual and had put out an extra thermos of hot water and additional tea. I picked up each container in turn to determine how full they were. Tom Brodsky, who I'd met at the horse ranch, stood next to a table talking to a short, balding man. As I straightened the silverware, Tom took a step closer to the person he was talking to.

"The festival was fine where it was until you came along," Tom said.

I could hear bitterness in his voice.

"Tom, we've been over this before. I made the suggestion, but the committee made the decision," the man responded.

"Right, Alexander. Like you had no influence. I saw you out and about, buying drinks and glad handing the members."

"Why are you so against moving the festival to Redwood Cove?"

"Fort Nelsen, where it's always been held, is a real fort and part of the Russian heritage we're trying to preserve. It's part of our history," Tom replied.

"It's also quite a ways out of town on a winding road many don't want to drive," Alexander argued. "We'll have a bigger turnout here. More people will have an opportunity to learn about our past, and we'll raise more money for the scholarships."

"And it will give attendees an opportunity to visit your shop. I've seen the ads you've placed in the paper here and in San Francisco. *Come to the Russian Heritage Festival and, while you're there, stop to see the fine Russian artifacts on display at Russian Treasures, located in the heart of Redwood Cove.*"

Alexander's face reddened. "I paid for those ads and have every right to mention my business."

"It's a store, not a museum," Tom snapped back.

"You're just angry because you didn't get your way," Alexander retorted. "Grow up."

"You're a newcomer. You come in and begin changing the way we've done things for years." Tom slammed down his teacup with such force, the contents splashed on the counter. I grabbed some napkins and began cleaning it up.

"I'm sorry, Kelly."

"No problem, Tom. I'll have it cleaned up in a jiffy."

Tom picked up his cup, wiped off the bottom with a napkin, and blotted the tea from the saucer. I tossed the napkins in the wastebasket near the sideboard, and Tom did the same. He turned to Alexander, as if to continue their argument.

Just as Tom opened his mouth, a tall, distinguished-looking man in a gray three-piece pin-striped suit entered the room. The silver flecks at his temples set off his dark hair. He carried a black leather briefcase.

Alexander lowered his voice and hissed, "Stop. Vladimir is here. He's been advertising the event in San Francisco and encouraging people to attend. He doesn't need to hear us hurling accusations back and forth."

The short man stepped away from Tom and waved at the newcomer. "Vladimir, glad to see you, my good friend."

"Same here, Alexander." Vladimir's voice carried a deep bass note. He walked over to where we stood and held out his hand to Alexander. Vladimir wore two large insignia rings, one on each hand, and his nails appeared smooth and well-cared for. "The day of the festival is almost upon us."

Alexander shook his hand and nodded. "The town is filling up already. To the best of my knowledge, there are no rooms available here or in nearby communities."

Alexander glanced in my direction. I had my name badge on, with its accompanying title of manager.

He approached. "Excuse me. I'd like to introduce myself. I'm Alexander Koskov."

"Kelly Jackson. Nice to meet you."

"I was just telling my friend here, there are no more accommodations available in town or nearby. Is that correct?"

"Yes, we've been turning down people's requests for several weeks now. The majority of them mentioned your festival."

Alexander smiled and rubbed his hands together. "Wonderful." He turned back to Vladimir. "I'm sure the work you've done promoting the event in San Francisco has a lot to do with the interest generated."

"Good. I like supporting local businesses, as well as giving people an opportunity to learn about our Russian heritage and what life was like for the early settlers. This has the added benefit of providing money for the education of our youth."

"Yes, Vladimir. So true," Alexander said.

Tom passed by me, muttering, "I know which business you're supporting, Alexander."

"Where are you staying, Vladimir?" Alexander asked.

"I have a room at Bellington Bed and Breakfast, near the festival grounds, along with a number of other committee members. We blocked some rooms there."

"Ah, yes, I'm familiar with it," Alexander said.

The newcomer gave a slight bow in my direction. "I am Vladimir Yeltsin, Ms. Jackson. It is a pleasure to meet you."

"Likewise," I replied. "The town is definitely buzzing. I suspect you'll have a great turnout."

He pulled a black leather wallet from his pocket, extracted a business card, and handed it to me. "If you have any questions about the festival, please feel free to call me."

"Thank you. I will. I'm new to the area and have a lot to learn."

"If you decide to visit San Francisco, I'd be happy to write down some Russian places of interest for you."

"That's a nice offer. I appreciate it. I do plan a visit there sometime soon."

I read his card. His company name was Golden Enterprises, and he was the president. The type of work was simply listed as investments.

Vladimir and Alexander wandered off and joined a group in the corner of the room.

Rudy and Ivan walked in. Ivan carried a large pot. It only took a few seconds for the earthy smell of beets to announce the arrival of the borscht he loved to make, though few in Redwood Cove chose to partake of it. He had an appreciative audience for his soup with this group; people filled glass mugs with the ruby red liquid.

Helen entered with a platter of baklava. The sweet smell of honey began to fill the room. Participants' eyes lit up. People quickly lined up to get a plate and delve into the delicious-looking pastry.

I headed toward a blond woman who I knew to be Alena Stepanova. She was about my height, which put her at five foot six, and was the person I worked with on plans for the meeting. Alena lived in San Francisco, so most of our conversations had been by phone. She wore a long black skirt, high-heeled green leather boots, and a short, cropped green wool jacket over a black top. Long red nails set off the white skin of the delicate hand holding her teacup. Her hair was shaped in a smooth, sleek style—big city smart all the way.

"Alena, is there anything else you need?"

"No, Kelly. You have everything so well organized." She nodded toward the crowd at the sideboard. "And Helen had me sample the baklava when I got here. Divine! We'll definitely book your room for future meetings. It'll be especially convenient for me because I can stay here at the inn."

"Where are you staying now?"

"I'm staying at the Bellington Bed and Breakfast, next to where the event will be held."

I pointed to the phone in the corner. "If you need anything, just dial. The number is written on it."

"Thanks." She got in line to help herself to more of the flaky dessert.

I joined Helen in the kitchen.

She held out a plate with a triangular piece of baklava on it. "Would you like to try it?"

"You bet." The fragile pastry almost melted in my mouth, leaving a luscious chewy mixture of honey, nuts, and spices.

Maybe its sweetness will take away some of the bitterness I heard between Tom and Alexander.

The meeting attendees departed about an hour and a half later. I helped Helen clean up the room. The baklava platter didn't even have any crumbs left on it.

I went back to my rooms to get my jacket. I'd been in all day, and a walk in the fresh air to the post office to mail some bills seemed like a good idea. My cell phone rang just as I reached for my coat. I recognized the number as Scott Thompson's, one of my colleagues. He was currently running the Redwood Cove Community Center.

"Hi, Scott."

"Hello, Kelly. As I recall, you said you were interested in learning how to make a pie during one of your cooking lessons."

Uh-oh.

I'd actually hoped he'd forgotten about that. My name and the word *cook* didn't belong together. After Scott prepared a gourmet dinner for me, our talk had turned to cooking, and he'd learned of my less-than-knowledgeable state in that department. He'd offered to teach me, and, at the time, it had sounded like a fun idea. Not so much now.

We'd had one lesson so far—mac and cheese. He said we'd start easy and no one could mess that up. Enter me. I didn't mean to prove him wrong. I like cheese, so it didn't bother me that the sauce had lumps of unmelted cheese and, personally, I liked supersoft, mushy pasta. I figured al dente was a fancy phrase for chewy and not completely cooked. Scott had patiently helped me through a second batch.

"How about another session, with apple pie on the menu?"

After watching Helen with the delicate dough, the thought of making a flaky crust caused a feeling of panic.

"Um, I'm really busy right now. We have a full house, and the Russian Heritage Festival is this weekend."

"Kelly, the event is just one day. Saturday. The pie will only take a couple of hours. Helen's there at the property to help guests. You wanted to prepare a pie for the Silver Sentinels because you didn't bake one for their pie party."

A chance for escape. "Yes, for one of their meetings. They don't have any scheduled that I know of."

"And we both know that can happen in minutes with a phone call."

Right. News got out so fast in a small community, it was like the telephone wires were hit with a magic wand.

"I'd be happy to call them," Scott said.

I just knew he was wearing his impish grin.

I sighed internally, thinking I might as well get it over with. "Okay. When do you want to get together?"

We settled on a date and time. I slipped into my jacket and headed out. On one hand, I looked forward to seeing him; on the other, a failed marriage had left me gun-shy about starting another relationship.

The crisp air refreshed me after all the paperwork. I mailed the bills and decided to take a circuitous route back to get more exercise and enjoy the sights of Redwood Cove. I saw Alexander's shop, Russian Treasures, and decided to go in. I hadn't visited it yet.

Alexander was busy behind a counter, with three women gathered around in front of him. He held up a lady's watch. "This is a replica of the Russian Imperial Grand Duchess's watch designed by Peter Carl Fabergé. The creator of this piece used crystals in place of the original watch's diamonds."

The stones rested on a black enamel circle around the clock face. The pattern of an X sparkled in the light on the top, bottom, and both sides. I wouldn't have known they weren't diamonds. My fashion-conscious sister would love something like that. I'd come back to do some shopping with her in mind.

I wandered around the shop. It was an eclectic mix of statues, embroidered pieces of material, clothes, and other odds and ends, which I assumed were all of Russian origin. A couple of intricately carved small boxes caught my eye.

Colorful stones embedded in the top of one formed the pattern of a star. The other one had inlaid swirls of a gold-colored metal. Mom collected ones like these for their beauty, as well as their practicality because they were suitable for jewelry or odds and ends. I took photos of them and their information cards and would ask her if she was interested in my buying the boxes for her.

I examined an interesting piece on the wall, a detailed religious metal sculpture. I glanced over at the counter. Alexander handed one of the women a wrapped package. He then headed in my direction as the women left the shop.

"Good to see you again, Ms. Jackson. Do you know what that piece represents?"

"It looks like the Mother of God praying over Jesus."

"You are correct. It is a Russian icon. Many of them were created, starting hundreds of years ago. The halo is gold leaf. The one you are looking at is from the early nineteenth century."

"What does a piece like this sell for?"

"This one has a price tag of four thousand two hundred dollars. Unscrupulous artists make them today and use aging techniques to make them appear antique. That one is genuine."

"It's beautiful," I said.

"Is there anything I can help you find?" Alexander asked.

"No. I just wanted to come in and see what was here."

"Welcome to Russian Treasures. If you have any questions, I'm happy to answer them." He walked off.

I went to the glass case, where the ladies had been standing. A large book rested open on the counter with photographs of gold coins. Prices were listed under them.

Alexander joined me. "I collect and sell gold coins. The prices you see there change regularly, based on what the current market value is for them."

"Interesting." I looked around. "You have a lovely store."

"Thank you. Stop by anytime," he said. "Unfortunately, my last helper was unreliable and I had to let him go. I haven't found a replacement yet, so sometimes the store won't be open. But I don't leave for long, and my return time will always be posted." He looked at the tall grandfather clock standing in the corner. "I do have to close early today. I'm meeting someone."

"Thank you again," I said.

I walked briskly back to Redwood Cove Bed and Breakfast. Helen was starting to put out the appetizers in the parlor. I joined her with a tray of wineglasses, then retrieved a bottle of chardonnay from the refrigerator and a merlot from the wine rack. I opened them and put the bottles next to the glasses.

I returned to my rooms, did some more paperwork, and was starting to think about dinner when my cell phone rang.

"Hello?"

"Kelly, I need your help."

I knew it was Rudy's voice, but there was a quavering quality to it I'd never heard before.

"Rudy, what's happened?"

"The police found a body on the *Nadia*."

"What! Who?"

"Alexander Koskov. He was shot."

Chapter 6

"The police want Ivan and me to go to the marina immediately," continued Rudy. "We could take the bus...but I'd like you to be there with us."

"I understand. I'm on my way."

Dinner would have to wait. I grabbed my purse and jacket. Helen was in the kitchen.

"Helen, I have to leave. Ivan and Rudy...have a problem. They need my help."

No need to mention what had happened until I knew more.

"Of course, Kelly. I'll take care of the inn. I'll bring over what I made for dinner, and Tommy and I can eat here."

"Thanks. I appreciate it."

I arrived at the Doblinsky brothers' house ten minutes later. They were waiting out front wearing heavy wool jackets. Wisps of fog were beginning to move in and were winding their way around the brothers and their home.

"So appreciate." Ivan placed himself in the back seat.

Rudy settled in the passenger seat. "Yes." He wrung his hands. "We do not know what is happening. The dagger, and now a man killed. Police questioning us again."

I drove onto the highway. "Deputy Sheriff Stanton is thorough and fair. He'll find out the truth." I glanced over at Rudy. "Everything will be okay."

The brothers were silent the rest of the trip. Long shadows of trees covered the parking lot in the last of the sunlight. Three police cars were parked at the far end nearest the marina. Two officers stood next to each other, talking. The droopy ears and face of Gus as he looked out the car window identified which vehicle was Deputy Stanton's. An officer held open the driver's side door of a coroner's van as he talked to Stanton.

I parked a little distance from the police cars. We all got out. The same smell of fish I had noticed yesterday filled the air, only now it was stronger.

I stood in front of Rudy and Ivan. "I want you both to take a deep breath. The police will get to the bottom of this, and they won't find either one of you there when they do."

They glanced at each other, worry lines marring their brows. Then I saw them each inhale deeply and square their shoulders. I fell in next to them as we marched more than walked to where the officers were.

Deputy Stanton turned toward us as the driver of the van got in and drove off. He looked at the brothers. "Do either of you know Alexander Koskov?"

They both nodded.

"He is on the Russian Heritage Committee and was at meeting today with us," Ivan said.

"When did you last see him?"

"When the meeting was over. He left with the rest of us," Rudy replied.

I'd seen him after that. "I saw him this afternoon at around three thirty. I stopped by his store out of curiosity. It was mentioned at the meeting, and I'd never been in the shop before."

"Did he say anything that might be helpful?" Stanton asked.

"He mentioned he had to close the shop early because he was meeting someone."

"Did he say who or where?"

I shook my head. "No. I didn't see him again after I left." I frowned. "How did you find out about the body?"

"Another anonymous phone call. Popular these days." He pulled out a notepad. "Rudy, Ivan, where were you between three thirty and five, which is when the call came in?"

"Both at home," Rudy said.

"Yah. We work on signs for the festival," Ivan added.

"We volunteered to help," Rudy explained.

"Did either of you come to the boat today?" Deputy Stanton asked.

"No. We do as you say and not come," Ivan answered.

Stanton scribbled a note, then closed his notepad and slipped it into his pocket. "I want you to go with me onto the boat one at a time to see if there is anything different. Both of you come with me now. One can wait on the dock."

Ivan's shoulders sagged, and he shuffled behind the officer. Rudy's face paled, and his feet seemed to drag, gravity pulling him to a slower pace.

I didn't follow them. I saw the same man I'd spoken to yesterday at the bait shop. Same position, same place, other than that he'd shifted his chair to catch the last sunbeam. Probably the same bib overalls.

As I approached, he tossed a chunk of bread to a group of gulls that had gathered near him. They were a type of bird I wasn't very familiar with, coming from Wyoming. I was always startled by how viciously they attacked each other for a morsel of food. I'd actually seen them lock beaks in midair.

"Hi, Joe."

"Hi back."

I guessed the police had already questioned him. Maybe he wouldn't mind telling me what he knew. It might help Ivan and Rudy.

He leaned back and hooked his thumbs in the straps of his overalls. "With the action you bring every time you show up, I ain't got no need to watch crime shows." His missing front tooth created a slight lisp. "A dagger. A body. What's next?"

I shook my head. "No idea. Hopefully, nothing. Did you see anyone on the boat? Notice anything that might be helpful?"

"Naw. Police asked the same thing. Had a few customers. Got a bite to eat. Probably happened then."

"Did you hear anything?"

"Nope."

"I wonder how they're getting in the boat," I mused.

"'Magine the same way you did."

I looked at him, startled. "What do you mean?"

"The key in the chest, a course."

"How do you know about that?"

"The brothers are nice guys but secretive they're not. Anyone watchin' them enter their boat would know where the key is."

Made sense, though that didn't help me any either.

"Have you seen any strangers around here?"

"Sure. Lots. Many of these boats take passengers out. The commercial ones are always hirin' new people. Workers come and go."

"Do you remember anything unusual about yesterday around the time when the dagger was found?"

"Nope. Same ol' same ol'."

Nothing. I saw the brothers heading back with Deputy Stanton. They stopped next to me.

Stanton took off his hat, ran his fingers through his hair, and replaced his Stetson. "That's all for now. Like I said before, don't go on the boat until you hear from me."

"Understood, Deputy Stanton," Rudy replied.

"A team of detectives is on the way to do a thorough search of the vessel. I'll keep you posted."

Stanton's phone rang, and he stepped out of our hearing to answer.

I thanked Joe for answering my questions, and the three of us walked slowly to my Jeep.

"Did either of you see anything different about the boat?" I asked.

They both shook their heads.

"The only thing were the lines showing where the body had been," Rudy said.

I thought for a moment. I wondered if he'd been killed there or somewhere else. "Deputy Stanton said he was shot. Was there any blood?"

Rudy became even paler. "Yes," he whispered.

Okay, if there had been no blood, it was possible the body had been disposed of on the boat. Even with the blood, he still could've been killed elsewhere.

"Did you smell anything to make you think a gun had been fired?"

Ivan nodded. "Yah. Uncle used to have guns. Remember smell."

It seemed he probably had been killed on the *Nadia*. But the bait shop owner hadn't heard anything. Why? And why was he on the boat? Was that where he planned to meet someone?

"Hold up," Deputy Stanton called out to us. He caught up with us and stared at Rudy. "You said you knew Mr. Koskov from the committee."

Rudy nodded, his face now ashen.

"Did you know him in any other way?"

"Ye...ye...yes," he stuttered. "I did some business with him."

"What kind of business?"

"I...I sold him some gold coins."

"Your name was found on a well-hidden ledger in Koskov's store. Clearly, he didn't want people to know about it. What was it about the business you were conducting with Alexander Koskov that he found it necessary to hide?"

Chapter 7

Rudy blanched even whiter and swayed a bit. "N…n…nothing illegal. Not know why information hidden."

"Were you planning to meet Alexander here?" Stanton asked.

"No…no." Rudy kept shaking his head from side to side. "We always get together at his store."

"Do you have any idea what Koskov was doing on your boat?"

Rudy hadn't stopped shaking his head. "No."

Stanton kept the questions coming. "Where did you get the coins?"

"Easier to show you," Rudy said. "Come to house."

Stanton tapped his notepad with his pen. "Okay. Let me talk to the other officers, then I'll be over."

We were a somber, silent group when we left the marina. I didn't ask any questions. They'd already had enough of those to answer. I pulled into their driveway but didn't get out when Rudy and Ivan did.

Rudy held the passenger door open, letting in the cold night air. "Kelly, aren't you coming in?"

I zipped up my jacket. "I don't know if I should. It's a police investigation."

"Please come in. We need you here. Please." It was a plea more than a request.

Fear shone from his eyes. "Okay. I'll stay unless Stanton kicks me out."

Rudy's breath came out in a rush. "Thank you. Come in. Come in."

Dusk had settled in, and Rudy flipped on the porch light after he opened the door. We gathered in the kitchen, and Ivan put on water for tea. An unwrapped loaf of sliced French bread rested on a cutting board.

Rudy gestured toward it. "We were beginning to make dinner when Deputy Stanton called."

"I was about to do the same when I heard from you," I responded.

Rudy put the slices of bread on a tray and pulled a tub of whipped butter and a jar of peanut butter from the refrigerator. He placed everything on the table. "Deputy Stanton will be here shortly. This will help tide us over," he said wearily.

Ivan put out plates and knives for us and followed them with a stack of napkins.

I spread a thick layer of peanut butter on a piece of bread. I paused and inhaled its rich scent. It brought back childhood memories. When I scraped a knee, Mom would follow the Band-Aid with a peanut butter and jelly sandwich. Suddenly, the world would seem okay again. True comfort food. I sighed. We could use some comfort right now.

I took a bite. The bread had begun to go stale from its exposure to air after being left out in the brothers' hurry to depart. Nevertheless, it helped to quell the hunger that had leaped out when I entered the kitchen and caught a whiff of the lingering smells of cooked food.

We had time to eat several pieces before a knock on the door ended our quick snack. Rudy went to answer it and returned with Deputy Stanton. He nodded at me but didn't ask me to leave. Ivan picked up our dishes and put them in the sink.

Stanton looked at Rudy. "What did you want to show me?"

Rudy opened a cabinet and took a small metal hooked rod off a peg. "Please, everyone, follow me."

He led us to the living room. Ivan pulled the coffee table in front of the couch to one side, being careful not to disturb the chess pieces. Rudy bent over and grabbed a corner of the area rug and dragged it to the opposite side, revealing a trapdoor. He attached the rod to a very small ring and pulled it up. We gathered around him.

Rudy took a small flashlight from his pocket. "Wait here until I have the lights on."

He turned on his light, and in its beam, dusty stairs disappeared into darkness. A few cobwebs adorned the corners of the steps.

Rudy descended and disappeared into the blackness. A few moments later, lights went on downstairs.

"Come. We go now." Ivan led the way, gripping a handrail on his right as he went down.

The stairs were steep, and I followed suit by holding tightly onto the wooden bar. Stanton was right behind me. We entered what appeared to be a storage area. There were numerous boxes labeled in Russian.

Rudy waited for us on the far side of the room. A massive embroidered tapestry hung on the wall behind him. Rich greens and browns were woven together on a cream-colored fabric. The scene showed a woman wearing an elaborate gown lounging on a couch. She was being waited on by several women, one of them offering her a cup. Brass rings attached at the top of the material held it suspended from a metal bar.

Rudy pulled the material back to one side, creating soft folds and revealing a metal door. A large wheel was in the center, with a metal handle to one side. Rudy dialed the centerpiece this way and that a few times and pulled on the handle. The door swung open with ease, despite the fact that it appeared to be over a foot thick and held six now-recessed metal rods. Only a fine-balanced and well-oiled piece of heavy equipment would operate that way.

He entered the room, flipped on the lights, and waved us in.

I entered the vault and gasped. I didn't know what I had expected, but the sight before me took my breath away. I heard a quick inhalation from Deputy Stanton. Intricate tapestries hung from the walls. Shelves held Russian icons similar to the one in Koskov's store, but these were covered in gems and appeared to be painted with gold. The silver dagger case sat among them. Other items sparkled and gleamed in the bright overhead light.

"Rudy…Ivan…" That was all I could manage to say.

"We display them to keep the old country and our relatives close to us," Rudy said. "The United States is our home, but these objects are part of our history and our ancestors' lives."

Ivan pointed to two dark green stuffed chairs, one with a knitted navy throw over its arm, and a table with a reading lamp in the corner. "Mother made the blanket as well as this cap." He picked up a matching woolen hat that had been nestled in a corner on a shelf. "This was my father's."

I walked over to the bookcase next to the sitting area. All the titles were in Russian. "Did you bring these with you when you left your home?"

"No," Rudy replied. "There was no room for books, and they were heavy. We've built the collection over the years we've been here."

Ivan replaced the hat. "Yah. Help us to keep our language."

"We come down and read, spend time with our ancestors, so to speak." Rudy gave a slight smile. "Sometimes it feels like they are with us."

Deputy Stanton cleared his throat.

Rudy knelt at one of two safes along the wall. He turned the knob several times, first one way and then the other, and swung the door open. Stacks of gold coins of different sizes filled the interior.

"This is what I wanted you to see, Deputy Stanton. These are what I was selling to Alexander."

Ivan knelt beside his brother, reached in, and removed a jewelry case. There were others in the safe.

He opened the box, pulled out a necklace, and caressed it with his callused hands. "This was Mother's. Gift from prince. Very special to her."

The sparkling stones in the store had been crystals. I had no doubt what glittered in front of me now were diamonds.

He replaced it carefully in the box and put it back in the safe.

Deputy Stanton had taken out his notepad. "What types of coins are they?"

"Many different ones. Depending on the market, the value varies." Rudy took a notebook out of the safe and handed it to the officer. "I have an inventory. I will make a copy for you."

Ivan bent over and closed and locked the safe.

"Let's go back upstairs, and I will tell you all over some hot tea," Rudy said.

I turned to go, then stopped and shuddered as I saw a black braided leather whip hanging to one side of the door. I felt Ivan's heavy hand on my shoulder.

"No. Not what you think. Never used to hurt animals unless attacked." He pulled it down and uncoiled it.

It must have been over six feet long. Small gold stars adorned the sides of the handle and a large gold star was embedded on the top. Clearly, another Russian treasure. I ran my fingers down the smooth, supple leather and shivered again, thinking of the harm it could inflict.

"Cossacks used them to protect themselves and their horses from wolfpacks when riding through the forest," Rudy said.

"Never use on their horses." Ivan put the whip back on its hook. "Some said they love horses more than wives."

A sword in its sheath had been mounted on the wall next to the whip. Another fine example of ornate workmanship with its engraved metal. The handle appeared to be a silver snake.

Ivan patted it. "Rudy got dagger, prince gave me sword."

The three of us trudged up the steep stairs, while Rudy stayed behind to lock up. In the kitchen, Ivan again put on water and pulled out the tea choices and mugs. He took out the blue-and-white tin of shortbread cookies I'd seen on my previous visit and placed it in the center of the table. I helped myself to one. Rudy was back by the time the kettle began to whistle.

Deputy Stanton flipped through the pages of the notebook. "I see this is more than an inventory. It looks like you have been tracking your sales."

"Yes. The transactions from the last couple of months were all with Koskov. I was using a dealer, Harvey Goldstein, in Fort Peter for years. I switched because Alexander offered better prices, and he had interested buyers in the Russian community of San Francisco as well as in Russia."

"How did your previous dealer feel about that?" Stanton asked.

"Upset. Unhappy. But this was about business. It's what Ivan and I live on."

Ivan filled the mugs with water. We made our tea choices and let the beverages steep. Rudy put a plate out for the tea bags.

"I assume what we saw downstairs came from the Russian aristocratic family you told us about," Stanton said.

"Correct," Rudy replied. "Our uncle was able to smuggle it out. The family had split the treasures and money among the three groups. Most of it came with us because we had more room and could move faster. Ivan and I had some gold coins sewn into the lining of our coats, but we were kids and didn't know anything about the treasure we were carrying."

Ivan took a sip from his steaming cup. "Yah. Not know until uncle dying."

Rudy nodded. "He wanted us to learn the value of hard work and not have money until our retirement years."

"He make cellar and special room when he build house," Ivan added.

"Deputy Stanton…" Rudy paused, then continued. "Ivan and I never talk about what you and Kelly saw to anyone. I only sell a few coins at a time. We don't want to attract anyone's unwanted attention."

Stanton nodded. "I can certainly understand that."

"I know you need information to solve your case. I trust you implicitly. However, please take no offense, but some of your colleagues might not be so careful."

Stanton frowned but nodded in agreement. "I understand. I won't say anything to anyone." He flipped through the notebook again. "Just give me a copy of your transactions with Koskov and then you can hold on to this. If I need anything else, I'll let you know."

"Thank you, Deputy Stanton. I'll make a copy now," Rudy said.

Rudy left while I nibbled on a cookie and finished the last of my tea. "Ivan, do the other Silver Sentinels know about what you have?"

"No. Nobody knows. Dangerous knowledge to have." Ivan took my empty mug. "If people suspect what is here, might injure someone to force them to tell."

"Your secret is safe with me," I said.

Rudy returned and handed a couple of papers to Stanton.

"Rudy, I don't believe you or Ivan killed Alexander Koskov. However, I have to ask you both not to leave the area until this is cleared up."

Once again, Rudy's face paled.

Deputy Stanton departed, and Rudy stared at me. "Kelly, I'm scared. I'm a suspect in a murder case."

My heart went out to him. I'd never been in his situation, but I could imagine the terror it would bring. My stomach clenched. We needed to get to the bottom of what was going on.

Chapter 8

Ivan put his hand on his brother's shoulder. "Stanton good man. He find truth."

"I agree with Ivan," I said. "And you know how much he cares for you and all of the Silver Sentinels."

Stanton called them his *crime-solving seniors*, always with affection in his voice. Gertie, one of the members, had been his fifth-grade teacher. She called him William, which he allowed no one else to do.

"I know," Rudy said. "But first the family knife and now a body on the boat...a man I did business with. What if someone is trying to frame me? What if they plant evidence in a way that points to me as the killer? If Deputy Stanton didn't take action, someone else would."

He had a point. I believed Stanton would find a way to help Rudy, but it might not be before he was put through some difficult times.

"Time for the Silver Sentinels," I announced.

Ivan nodded. "Yah. We solve cases for others. Now it is our turn."

Rudy's tense face relaxed a bit. "You're right. We need to meet with our friends and get busy. We've solved other crimes. Now we can all work together to find out what's happening. We've done it before, and we can do it again."

I smiled. I was an honorary member of the group, because I didn't have the required silver hair for membership. I'd worked with them a number of times now on various cases. They were efficient and smart and had numerous connections in the area because of the many years they'd lived in Redwood Cove. Time to get the group involved.

"I'll go back to the inn and check the conference room schedule. I'll text everyone about when we can use it. Are both of you available tomorrow?"

They nodded. We said our good-byes, and I drove back to the bed and breakfast. It was past ten. I checked the fire in the parlor, and it was almost out. Only a few glowing embers remained to be seen behind the closed screen. Helen had put away the dishes and gotten the breakfast baskets out for tomorrow morning.

I went to the conference room. There were no meetings scheduled for the next day. I suspected the group knew about the knife and probably about the body, knowing how fast news traveled in our small town. I texted them, suggesting we meet at ten, but I let them know the day was open if there was a better time.

I retired to my quarters. Glancing toward the kitchen, I thought about dinner, then realized I wasn't hungry. The peanut butter sandwiches and cookies had filled me up.

I was tired and thought I'd go to sleep right away, but that didn't happen. I tossed and turned, thoughts and questions bouncing in my head. How and why had the knife and body ended up on the Doblinskys' boat? Who was responsible?

Finally, sleep crept over me, my dreams full of images of Russian treasure.

* * * *

I checked my phone the next morning. All the Sentinels had responded that ten would work.

I found Helen in the kitchen, working on the breakfast baskets. She routinely came in early to get coffee going for the guests.

"Did everything work out okay with Rudy and Ivan?" she asked.

"Not exactly. The police found a murdered man on the brothers' boat."

Helen had been about to reach for a cup. Her hand stopped in midair, and she jerked around. "Someone was murdered?"

I filled her in about what had been discovered, and that the brothers had been questioned. I left it at that. I trusted Helen, but I'd made a promise to Ivan and Rudy regarding their treasure. I also didn't know if Stanton wanted us talking about Rudy's gold coin sales.

Helen and I were putting the final touches on the guests' breakfasts when a deputy sheriff's car drove by the side window. I walked to the back door and looked through the glass. Deputy Stanton's large frame emerged from the car. He opened the back door of the vehicle and Gus slid more than jumped out.

He looked like a droopy version of Fred. Long ears, loose skin, sagging jowls, and an ever-wagging tail.

I opened the back door. "Good morning…Bill."

It would take a while to get used to calling him that after all the cases when I'd called him Deputy Stanton…and I'd be going back to that title shortly. I decided not to tip him off that the Silver Sentinels were about to launch. He'd find out soon enough. He didn't need anything else on his mind.

He and Gus entered. "Hi, Kelly. You're using my first name, so I'm assuming you and the Silver Sentinels aren't sleuthing right now."

"Right."

That would change later that morning.

"Good." He turned to Helen. "Thanks for offering to take care of Gus for me."

"No problem. Fred just lies around waiting for Tommy all day. Gus and Fred play together really well. The exercise and activity are good for him." She reached for a mug. "Do you have time for coffee?"

Stanton checked his watch. "I have about fifteen minutes."

Helen handed him a steaming cup of dark brown French roast.

"I've got meetings all morning," Stanton said. "We're finalizing plans for the festival. Along with tourists come pickpockets and thieves. Our car break-ins skyrocket. Then another meeting to discuss a new case." Stanton shot a glance at me.

"I filled Helen in about the body on the boat. She covered for me while I went to help the brothers, and I wanted to let her know what was going on. Helen knows about the knife as well."

Stanton nodded. "It's an unusual situation, for sure. I have no idea if the murder and the knife are connected. The only two things they have in common are the boat and Rudy."

The door flew open, and Tommy bounded in with Fred bouncing behind. "Hi, Deputy Stanton."

"Hey, Tommy. How are you today?" Stanton asked.

Tommy dropped his backpack on the floor by the counter and clambered onto the stool next to the officer. Fred and Gus touched noses and wagged a greeting, then settled next to their respective person.

"Great! We're having a math contest today. I love math!"

"Tommy, you need to leave for school in five minutes," his mother reminded him.

"I know."

"Do you have any projects coming up you'd like help with?" Stanton asked. "I enjoyed doing the science one with you."

"Not right now. There's supposed to be a big history assignment starting next month."

"Okay. Let me know when, and I'll put time aside to work with you." He sipped his coffee. "Since we won't be doing any schoolwork, how would you like to come to watch Gus in training?"

"Cool! Can Allie come, too?"

Allie was Daniel Stevens's daughter. He managed a sister property called the Ridley House, and we shared some of the chores associated with running the inns. Tommy was far beyond his fifth-grade level in math and science and was able to tutor eighth-grade Allie.

The two kids had become good friends. Tommy's Asperger's had made it difficult for him to fit in socially when he and his mother moved to Redwood Cove not long ago. Allie had made a big difference in Tommy's adjusting to the town.

"Sure," Stanton replied.

"Oh, boy. I'll text her." He reached for his phone.

"Not now. You need to get going," his mother said.

"Okay, Mom." He knelt on the floor and gave Fred a hug around his thick neck. "I'm coming home right after school today, Fred."

The hound grinned as if he understood.

"Bye, Deputy Stanton. Thanks for inviting me to watch you train Gus."

"You're welcome."

"Love you, Mom," he said over his shoulder as he grabbed his bag.

Tommy was out the door and on his bike in a flash. Sometimes I got tired just watching the speed at which he moved.

"Thanks for the coffee, Helen," Stanton said. "I'll be back around noon for Gus."

"Okay. See you then."

We finished preparing and delivering the baskets. As we cleaned up the kitchen, I told her the Sentinels were meeting at ten. She assured me she'd have refreshments ready. I went to my rooms and prepared a quick breakfast of cereal. When I saw it was nine thirty, I left for the conference room. The Silver Sentinels were usually early.

I put several sheets of chart paper on the wall and pulled out thick felt pens. Helen entered with a pitcher of ice water and set it on the sideboard next to the row of glasses we kept there, along with coffee cups.

She pulled a wooden box containing a tea selection from one of the drawers. "The coffee's brewing. I'll bring it in shortly, along with hot water for tea and a plate of fruit."

"Thanks, Helen."

The Professor was the first to arrive. He was a slight man with neatly trimmed silver hair. He took off his brown tweed cap and put it next to the place he usually occupied at the table. He straightened his bow tie, then turned to me. “So…I understand we have a murder to solve.”

Chapter 9

I wasn't surprised the Professor knew about the murder, but it was always interesting to learn how the communication system worked.

"How did you hear about what happened?"

"There's a fish market at the marina. I stopped there to buy some salmon for dinner last night. They have a coffee area, and Joe from the bait shop was holding court."

Puzzled, I asked, "What do you mean?"

"Seems he's become the unofficial crime scene reporter for the area. Had quite the group listening to him talk."

Remembering some of the comments he made to me, I warily asked, "What did he have to say?"

The Professor pursed his lips. "Let me see if I can remember his exact words." He paused for a moment. "*Can't wait to see what happens the next time that pretty lil redheaded gal shows up. Live action—much better than television.*"

The familiar warmth of a blush crept up my face. "I hate to disappoint him, but I have no plans for providing him with any more entertainment."

The Professor nodded. "There's certainly been enough going on."

"Yes, Rudy and Ivan are very worried."

"I can certainly understand why… a murdered man on their boat," he said.

"And a knife possibly covered with blood," I added.

The sound of female voices in the hallway preceded the arrival of Mary Rutledge and Gertie Plumber. Mary had a purse slung over one shoulder and what I knew to be a dog carrier over the other. She carried a plastic container.

The Professor stepped forward. "Let me help you."

"Thanks," Mary huffed, sounding a bit breathless, her plump cheeks rosy. Sparkling rhinestones glittered on the shoulders of her white fuzzy sweater.

He took the plastic box and placed it on the table. Mary deposited her purse next to a chair and placed the pink carrier on the one next to it. She unclipped the top and a brown Chihuahua head popped up. Princess had arrived.

Mary picked up her pride and joy, gave her a hug, then placed the dog on the floor. The little dog came over to greet me. Today's color theme for her fleece coat and jeweled collar was dark green. Two heart-shaped charms dangled next to her dog tags. I gave her a couple of pats on the top of her head and then she went to see what kind of attention the Professor would give her.

I took small plates out of the cabinet and placed them next to the napkins. Helen came in with thermoses of coffee and hot water and a platter of fruit. Mary took a tiny bed out of the closet. The Sentinels met here regularly, and I had told her she could store a dog bed in the room. Mary put it next to her chair, and Princess quickly claimed her space.

Mary pulled the lid off the plastic box. "I've been wanting to try this recipe for ages. Peanut butter and chocolate bars with dark chocolate frosting."

I poured a cup of coffee and took a sip, enjoying the strong brew. It was a dark organic roast from Mountain Mike's and smelled divine. I checked out Mary's treats and saw layers of peanut butter laced through chocolate.

Peanut butter. Chocolate. Coffee. My three favorite food groups. I picked up one of the bars, took a bite, and savored the sweet flavors.

More voices in the hallway, one with a deep, loud, booming tone, Ivan, heralded the arrival of the rest of the group. People greeted each other, prepared their drinks, got their snacks, and settled at the table. Rudy placed a worn leather satchel next to where he was going to sit.

Gertie leaned her cane against the wall. Even though she was only five feet two, she was no one you wanted to mess with. A retired schoolteacher, she kept the group organized and on task.

Gertie rapped on the table with her recently purchased gavel. "Ten. Time to get started. Rudy and Ivan, Kelly texted you need our help."

Rudy nodded. "I am worried…more than that…frightened. A dagger connected to me had what might be dried blood on it, and a man I did business with was murdered. Both were found on the *Nadia*."

The Professor twirled his pen. "Please fill us in on the details."

Rudy picked up his briefcase and placed it on the table. "I will start with the knife."

With that, he opened the bag and pulled out the case he'd shown us at his home. Unclasping the lid, he opened it, took out his dagger, like the one found on the boat, and placed it on the table.

Mary's hand flew to her throat. "Oh, my," she gasped.

I didn't know if her reaction was because of the fierce-looking blade, the almost blinding sparkle of the jewels, or both. I had looked at the one on the boat but hadn't really examined the weapon any further at Rudy's home. With it being the center of attention and resting by itself on the table, I got a second chance to inspect it. It hadn't lost any of its outstanding beauty.

"Well," the Professor said, "uh...that's quite a piece." He seemed at a loss for words.

"Rudy, are those jewels real?" asked Gertie.

"Yes," he replied. "I will tell you the story."

He proceeded to share with them what he had told Stanton and me—the brothers' life story. Gertie and the Professor took notes. Mary jotted down a few things, but her glance kept sliding to the dagger. Rudy didn't mention the money or the treasure. He finished, and the group was silent, absorbing what they'd learned.

Mary appeared a little teary-eyed. "Thank you for sharing your story, Rudy. I'm so sorry you were never reunited with your family."

"Yes, it's a real pity," the Professor said.

Rudy nodded. "Thank you."

"I think our first goal," Gertie said, "is to find out how the knife got on the boat. Let's start a chart."

"Good idea, Gertie." The Professor stood, picked up a felt-tip pen, and went to one of the pieces of paper I'd tacked on the wall. He put *knife* at the top and proceeded to add information gleaned from Rudy's tale.

"Rudy, I know you said you searched for your relatives in the past. Have you continued to do so?" I asked.

"Yes. Not like in the beginning or when the Internet became such an important means of communication, but I still search for their names on a regular basis."

"Maybe when we find out what is on the blade, that will give us some indication of what direction we should go to get information," the Professor said.

He wrote *substance on blade* with a question mark.

"Stanton said he'd let Rudy know as soon as he found out," I volunteered.

"Let's move on to the murdered man," Gertie said. "What can you tell us about him?"

"His name was Alexander Koskov," Rudy replied. "I sold him gold coins."

The Professor duly titled another chart.

"On his deathbed, our uncle revealed he'd been able to get some of the family gold out of Russia," Rudy said. "He had kept the money hidden so we'd have it for our retirement."

Mary picked up one of her chocolate bars and began nibbling on it. "How thoughtful of him."

"A good planner," Gertie added. "You were very fortunate."

"Yah," Ivan said. "Not get rich or have retirement plan from fishing."

"I have been selling the most valuable ones first, so I could keep my number of trips to the gold buyer to a minimum," Rudy said.

"Smart," the Professor said. "I can understand why you wouldn't want people to get wind of your money."

"I was using a dealer in Fort Peter, Harvey Goldstein, until recently. I trusted him in terms of being fair and not talking to people about the gold, but Alexander offered me a significantly better deal. We had coffee together and talked about Russia. He seemed like a nice person. I decided I'd give him a try. I downplayed what I had. Said I'd inherited a few coins recently."

The Professor noted *coin buyer* on the murdered man's chart.

"How did the other dealer feel about you not using him anymore?" Mary asked

"He was not pleased. Quite upset, actually."

The Professor added Harvey Goldstein to the list. "I think we should consider him a suspect, so I'll underline his name."

"There's more," Rudy said. "I received a call from Deputy Stanton asking if I knew someone by the name of Clay Johnson. His name was in Koskov's ledger, and he'd been selling coins like mine."

"Do you know him?" Gertie asked.

Rudy shook his head. "No. I think we should put his name on Alexander's chart in case we find out something more about him."

The Professor added the information as requested.

"I have another name you can add as a suspect," I said. "I heard Tom Brodsky arguing with Alexander about the location of the festival, and accusing him of doing it to better his business. He was very angry."

"Tom has been in charge of the festival for a long time," Gertie said. "I used to help him organize the different groups he had coming in. He was very proud of the event."

The Professor wrote his name and underlined it. "Anything else we can add to the list?"

"I saw Alexander not long before he was killed," I said. "He mentioned having recently fired an employee, but he didn't give a name."

The information went on the chart.

I continued, "I learned at the Russian Heritage Committee meeting that Alexander was working with a man named Vladimir Yeltsin from San Francisco. They seemed on good terms, so I don't consider him a suspect."

The Professor wrote Vladimir's name; then we looked at what he'd recorded on the lists.

"Let's start a Next Steps chart," Mary said.

The Professor posted another piece of chart paper on the wall.

"I don't see what else we can do with the knife," Gertie said. "I know the mother of Harvey Goldstein, the dealer you used to use. She's a member of my organic gardening club. I promised I'd give her some compost. I'll call to make plans to have her come over to my house to get it. I can strike up a conversation with her."

Mary chimed in. "She's in my church group. I can be with you having coffee when she arrives. You know, as if I just dropped in. I might be able to think of some questions as well."

"And I can talk to the owner of the store Koskov was leasing," the Professor said. "We've been friends for years, meet for coffee regularly, and occasionally go to musical events together. Maybe he can give us some background on Alexander, and he'll probably know the fired employee's name."

"I'll question Vladimir," I said. "He gave me his card and offered to make a list of Russian places for me to visit in San Francisco. He also encouraged me to get in touch with him if I had questions about the festival."

"Good thinking," Gertie said. "It sounds like he can give you some background on Koskov if you can get him to talk about Alexander."

"He's staying at an inn next to where they're setting up for the event. I'll call him and tell him I've been wanting to see the area and am planning to visit it soon. I'll ask if there's a good time for us to meet to talk about the festival while I'm there. When we get together, I'll ask him if he heard about Alexander being murdered. That, hopefully, will lead to some information."

We looked at the charts once more. The Professor had filled in our plans of what we were going to do.

"So little," Ivan muttered loud enough for us all to hear.

"What do you want us to do?" Rudy's tone and face spoke discouragement.

I frowned, hesitating to say what I was thinking, though I knew what I needed to do. "Rudy, it looks like this business is more connected to you than Ivan. However, we're dealing with a murdered man and a dagger. I don't like to say it, but it's possible you both might be in some danger."

"But why?" Rudy exclaimed.

"I don't know why, but I do know there's been violence and you seem to be at the center of it." I looked at him. "We don't know if someone might try to harm you in some way. I think you should lay low."

Ivan's brow creased. "How do that? Stay in bed?"

"Sorry, Ivan," I said. "That's an idiom that means to stay out of sight as much as possible. It's not a good time to go out and question people."

"Yes. I remember idioms. I call idiotgrams at first," he responded.

We all laughed. Teaching him idioms had been fun.

The light moment amid all the gloom released some tension.

"I agree with Kelly," the Professor said. "We don't know why all of this has happened. You and Rudy need to be careful."

"I agree as well," Gertie said. "I think it would be even better if you could be with friends whenever possible. That would give you an alibi if anything else happens, and help keep you safe."

Rudy looked shocked. "Something else?"

Mary got up, walked over to him, and gave him a hug. "We have a saying, 'better safe than sorry.' None of us think anything else is going to happen, but the fewer chances you take, the better."

Rudy sighed. "The chess club is meeting in the town hall this afternoon. I can go hang out there."

"That sounds perfect," the Professor said.

"Ivan usually doesn't play, though." He looked at his brother. "It could be boring for you."

"I go where you go," Ivan said. "Not let anyone hurt you."

"They usually have Russian newspapers and magazines," Rudy commented.

"Yah. I enjoy. Keeps me knowing about Russia today."

Gertie gave an affirmative nod. "Okay. We have our assignments. Let's see what we can find out."

"When do you want to meet next?" I asked.

"Tomorrow, if possible," the Professor said. "Let's move as fast as we can on this. Even if we haven't spoken to everyone we want to see, we'll pool what knowledge we have."

We found a time when we could all meet in the afternoon. Mary gathered up Princess and her box of goodies. Rudy put the knife in its case and then into the worn satchel. People said their good-byes and left.

I put the dirty dishes on a tray and ferried them to the kitchen. I then retrieved the thermoses.

Helen came in as I was finishing cleaning up. "How did the meeting go?"

"We have some ideas of where we can gather more information. That's all we can do at this point. How are the dogs?"

"Snoozing in the sun after playing."

"I'm going over to the community center for a while this afternoon. I'll be back in plenty of time to help with the evening appetizers."

I didn't mention that I was going to bake a pie…or attempt to.

My cell phone rang, and I saw it was Rudy.

"What's up?" I hoped it wasn't yet another find on the *Nadia.*

"Deputy Sheriff Stanton called." He paused. "The red substance on the knife isn't blood."

Chapter 10

"What is it then?" I asked.

"He said it's fake blood, like they use in the movies and plays," Rudy replied.

What on earth? This case kept getting stranger and stranger. "Well, that must be a relief for you. There's no evidence the dagger was used in foul play."

"Correct. Now, the question is how it got there and who had it."

"Why don't you text the group? That will give them some time to digest this new piece of information before tomorrow's meeting."

"Good idea," Rudy replied. "See you then."

I gave Helen the news just as Stanton's car drove in. I waved to him through the window of the back door and gestured for him to come in.

"Hi," I greeted him. "Rudy just called with the good news about the substance on the dagger not being blood."

"Yeah. I'm glad there's no indication it was used in a crime. Now we just have to decide what to do with it."

"What do you mean?"

"It's clear it belonged in Rudy's family at one time, but he wasn't the one who possessed it. We need to see if we can find the owner."

"If his sister or brother come forward, it'll be easy for you to identify them. But if they sold it or someone stole it…anyone could try to claim it."

Stanton groaned. "Please, don't go there. I know what you're saying. We'll cross that bridge if and when we come to it. We've put a partial description of the knife on Facebook and Twitter. We're also doing a search for the names Rudy gave us. We have a lot of resources Rudy doesn't have access to."

"I hope you find his relatives...Deputy Stanton."

The officer's eyebrows shot up. "So, we're back to using formal names? Does this mean what I think it does?"

I nodded. "The Sentinels and I met this morning. We all have our assignments."

He sighed. "I know I can't stop you. I know you know to be careful. And I know you'll keep me in the loop with anything you find out, right?"

"Yes, we will."

He turned to Helen. "I'll pack up Gus and be off. Thanks again for tending him."

"My pleasure. You might have trouble waking him. He and Fred were both snoring up a storm while basking in the sun."

We shared a laugh and Stanton departed.

Helen pulled a box out of the refrigerator and put it on the counter.

It was phyllo dough. "People really liked your baklava. I heard lots of appreciative comments."

"Apparently so. I've been asked to make it again, only twice as much this time."

She pulled a sheet off the stack. The paper-thin dough was almost translucent. Despite her extreme care, one of the sheets tore. The next one did as well. My thoughts darted to my impending pie crust. I was a jinx just standing near anything having to do with pastries.

Nope.

I didn't feel ready for this.

Maybe I could convince Scott to let me buy the pie crust this time. I went to my room and called him.

"Hi, Kelly. What's up?"

"I was just watching Helen make baklava—"

"Oh, do you want to make that instead? I just happen to have—"

"No!" I didn't mean to shout. Panic made me do it. "Sorry. I didn't mean to be so loud. Even as good a cook as she is, it was falling apart at times. Probably because I was close to it."

"Kelly, you had nothing to do with it ripping. Even the best chefs tear it."

"I was wondering if I could buy a frozen crust and just work on the filling this time."

"Kelly..." Scott paused. "I'll tell you what. Let's do this. You can do the filling with me guiding you each step of the way. Then we'll work as a team on the crust. It won't be me just instructing you."

It wasn't the answer I was hoping for, but I wasn't surprised, and it was a good compromise.

"Okay. Please don't be upset if it doesn't turn out."

"No worries there. Besides, I have all the ingredients we need to make as many pies as necessary until we get the results we want."

My inner groan was louder than the one Stanton had issued earlier. "Oh, good." Those were the heaviest lighthearted words I think I'd ever uttered.

"I'll see you in an hour, then," Scott said.

We ended the call. I fixed a sandwich and ate it at the desk in my quarters while I checked the registrations for next week. After that, I wrote down a few festival questions for Vladimir Yeltsin and called him. He didn't answer, so I left a message.

When it was time to go, I took out my Jeep keys and said good-bye to Helen on my way through the kitchen. I was tempted to ask her to wish me luck. As I sat in the driver's seat, a text alert sounded from my phone.

I checked, and there was a message to the group from the Professor. The fired employee's name was Rick Stapleton. The lease agreement listed Alexander as the manager and the owner as the Williams Corporation. Oddly, there were two sets of surveillance cameras. One was obvious and meant to alert customers they were being filmed. The other set was well hidden and seemed to be aimed mostly at where the employees worked.

I thought about this new information on the way to see Scott. Alexander didn't own the shop which was the impression I'd gotten at the meeting. The hidden cameras seemed to indicate the owner wanted to keep tabs on the employees. Had something happened to create distrust? I'd ask Daniel if he knew Stapleton. We'd figure out the next steps regarding the Williams Corporation at the next meeting. I put investigation thoughts aside as I pulled into the parking lot.

Scott had developed and now managed the Redwood Cove Community Center, which was only about ten minutes away inland. It was the brainchild of our boss, Michael Corrigan. He had wanted to give something back to the community, as well as reach out to homeless or struggling veterans in the area. To that end, a variety of classes, ranging from organic gardening to nutrition, had been created. Cottages had been built for the veterans. They lived onsite and were getting whatever assistance was germane to their situation.

Living at the community center with only the small town of Redwood Cove nearby had been a big change for Scott. He had traveled extensively all over the world for Resorts International to solve problems as they arose. Scott loved the job as well as the big city excitement he encountered as he went from place to place.

When Michael decided to build the center, he'd offered the job of creating it to Scott. It would require months to build. I was surprised when Scott accepted. He had told me he wanted to experience what living in the area would be like. Besides, he'd added with a grin, he could experiment with new recipes.

As I parked, one of the new shuttle buses pulled in and stopped at the front of the building. A half a dozen men and women disembarked, all chattering happily and smiling.

I knew classes had started last week but hadn't looked at the schedule yet. The Silver Sentinels had been on the committee to create the center and decide what would best fit the needs of the Redwood Cove residents.

I followed them in the front entrance. They were met by a tall man I knew to be Jim Patterson, the master gardener. Overstuffed chairs and couches, all draped with colorful soft throws, filled the lounge they were in. A variety of magazines were stacked on end tables. A fire burned in the large fireplace. The room was designed to make people feel comfortable and relaxed, and it succeeded admirably.

I went on through to the commercial-size kitchen and stopped. The large island in the center was filled with pots, bowls, measuring cups, and various implements I didn't recognize. Two glass containers with screw-on lids held what I suspected was sugar and flour. A bag of apples was next to the sink. This was a big project in the making, and I was the one who would be doing it. Why had I ever suggested a pie? I had survived my first lesson of mac and cheese, sort of, but this was a whole different ball game.

Scott wasn't in the room, so I decided this was a good time to go see the llamas the center had purchased for their wool, which would be used in a weaving class. I knew bags of llama snacks were in the refrigerator. I grabbed a few and fled as quickly as I could, lest Scott returned and the baking started.

I went out the back door to the pasture, where the herd of five females grazed. The Silver Sentinels and I had named them. We didn't own them, but we referred to them as *our llamas*.

Rudy and Ivan had named the large white one Natasha, after a Russian snow queen. The Professor had added a literary touch and named his black one Louisa May, in honor of Louisa May Alcott. Nell, the tan one, represented Gertie's aunt, and the butterscotch one answered to Miss M, the moniker Mary and her sister, Martha, had decided upon.

I called out, "Annie! Annie!"

A brown-and-white-spotted head shot up on a long, slender neck and looked in my direction. She immediately headed for me. I pulled a carrot from one of the bags I'd snatched from the kitchen. I held it out and she gently took it from my hand. I ran my fingers through her soft, tight reddish curls. They were the reason I'd decided to name her after Orphan Annie.

The other llamas weren't to be left out, and soon all five lined the fence and I doled out my treats.

"Kelly, I'm back," Scott said from the back door.

I gave each one a last pet, took a deep breath, squared my shoulders, and turned. There he was, Mr. Tall, Dark, and Handsome. My thought was a cliché, but it just fit some men perfectly and Scott was one of them. I followed him into the kitchen.

"Sorry for not being here. I had to step out to help one of the veterans with some boxes. He just moved in."

"How many are living here now?"

"Six men and two women," Scott said. "They're all involved in training post-traumatic stress disorder dogs for veterans. They received good news last week. Michael said they could have dogs of their own as long as they passed the Canine Good Citizen program."

My boss loved dogs and believed they helped people live fuller lives. I agreed with him.

"Wonderful! A while back, one of the men mentioned he hoped that would happen. I know Michael allows employees to have dogs on the Resort International properties if they pass the test."

Scott rubbed his hands together. "Let's get started. This will be fun."

Fun *was a subjective word. I wasn't sure it fit here at all.*

I put on the apron Scott offered, washed my hands, and rolled up my sleeves. The project began.

Peeling the apples was a cinch, because I'd peeled a lot of potatoes on the ranch. Scott showed me how to use an apple corer, and he had a nifty metal straight-edge tool for leveling off spices. I was beginning to feel more confident.

Then came the crust.

A short while later, I had flour on my face, flour footprints dotted the floor, and the once-neat counter looked like a train wreck—one that had been carrying a load of flour. Scott had said toss a handful of flour on the pastry board. So, I'd scooped up a bunch and thrown it on the board. How was I to know it would create a white cloud? And I didn't realize how far it could travel with one small toss. Knocking over the jar of flour hadn't helped the situation.

I sneezed once, twice...and kept on sneezing.

Scott handed me some tissues. "Here you go. Let me show you how to flour the board."

He demonstrated, and I learned that he meant a little flour in my palm, not a fistful, and *toss* meant to gently place the flour on the board.

"I'm so sorry for the mess. I'll clean it up." I dashed for the sink and grabbed a sponge. I turned and headed for the island.

"Kelly, wait!" Scott shouted.

Startled, I slid to a stop on the powdery floor.

"Don't you remember making glue in elementary school? It was flour and water. That's not the first step in cleaning this up."

My heart was beating faster. I was such a dunce. "I'm sorry. I wasn't thinking."

I grabbed the wastebasket from the corner and began sweeping the flour into it with my hand in swift, jerky movements.

Scott started to walk by me. "I'll get the vacuum."

Just then, I accidentally pushed the flour container off the counter. As it began to fall, I made a grab for it, as did Scott. I managed to get hold of it and held it up in a sweeping motion, causing another dreaded white cloud. This time it floated into Scott's face.

His dark eyebrows were now frosted white, as was part of his hair.

I couldn't suppress the laugh that came welling up. "You'll make a very distinguished Silver Sentinel."

His eyebrows rose in a questioning manner, and he went to look at himself in a mirror on the broom closet door.

He turned. "Well, at least as a member I can keep an eye on all of you."

This time we both burst out laughing.

Scott cleaned himself up, and we worked together on the floor. When that was done, he kept his word and helped in making the crust. He handled some of the delicate finishing touches, like doing the final rolling out of the crust and transferring it to the pie pan. He showed me how to crimp the edges, and I managed to do it successfully, if not exactly making it look pretty as I squished the soft dough between my fingers.

"I'm really sorry about the mess," I said.

Scott shook his head. "No problem. You know you've been baking when a little flour sifts into your life. You didn't do badly for your first time out."

I knew he was being kind. We cleaned up the kitchen, and it was in decent shape by the time the pie began to fill the kitchen with a wonderful aroma. We sat in the window seat, sipping coffee, while waiting for our creation to be done.

"So, what's been happening this week?" he asked.

I emitted another inward groan. Scott didn't like what the Silver Sentinels and I did in terms of solving crimes because of his concern we might get hurt. He respected our right to do it and understood our reasons, but it was a sensitive subject.

The local newspaper only came out once a week, and the murder had happened after the latest edition. Scott, being new to the area, wasn't connected to the communities' lightning-swift communication chain. I was sure he had no idea what was coming.

How did I tell him we were trying to solve a murder?

Chapter 11

The timer went off and gave me a few moments to gather my thoughts. Scott signaled me to follow him to the oven. He opened the door, and we peeked in.

"Perfect," he said.

The delicious smell of warm apple pie and spices was making my mouth water. Maybe there was something to this baking bit after all.

"I want you to do the honors of taking it out." He handed me oven mitts and pointed to a cooling rack on the counter.

I slipped on the mitts, opened the oven door, and reached in for the pie. Pulling it out, I turned and placed it on the rack. Juice bubbled out of the slits on top of the evenly browned crust.

"It needs to cool," Scott said. "Now, where were we?"

I was trying to figure out how to tell you I'm investigating a murder case with the Silver Sentinels.

The answer was to just tell him.

"Actually, there's been quite a lot going on."

I went on to share with him about the dagger, the murdered man, and Rudy's fear at being questioned by the police because of his connections to the dead man. I shared Rudy and Ivan's life story. I told him everything I'd told the Sentinels. "The Sentinels and I met this morning and put together a plan to gather information."

Scott's lips had increasingly tightened as I shared what I knew. "We've talked a number of times about what you and the others are doing, so I won't do it again. It's always hard knowing you and the Silver Sentinels are involved in crime solving and possibly putting yourselves in danger. If there's any way I can help, please let me know."

The tension that had built up in me as I told the story and saw his expression change began to dissipate. My shoulders, which had inched up a bit, now relaxed into their normal position. I appreciated the fact that he wasn't the lecturing kind. He'd said his piece a while back. He knew I didn't need to be reminded.

The smile that had been part of his face during our baking escapade had vanished.

I put my hand on his arm. "Scott, you know we'll be careful."

"I know."

"And this is something we need to do to help our friends."

"I know." His face was still grim.

I spied a computer on a small desk in the corner and came up with what I thought was a brilliant plan—change the subject. "Are you going to go to the Russian Heritage Festival?"

"I'll definitely check it out. I read about it in last week's paper, and it sounds like there'll be many unusual events."

"I haven't had a chance to look at the schedule. Let's check it out while the pie cools," I suggested.

"Sounds like a good idea—and a better subject to discuss than the one we were on."

I wasn't as clever as I thought. Scott knew exactly what I was doing.

Scott went over and picked up the laptop and put it on the table. We slid our chairs into position to be able to look at it together. He typed in *Russian Festival Redwood Cove* and up popped the event's website. Scott clicked on *Activities*, and the schedule came into view.

"The Russian Heritage Committee met at the inn," I said. "I heard people at the meeting talking about the festival's purpose. They want people to learn about what Russian life was like for the early settlers."

"I see ongoing demonstrations by blacksmiths, spinners, weavers, broom makers, woodworkers, and many other craftspeople. Sounds like fun."

I pointed to the screen. "There's a free horse-drawn wagon ride. I bet Tommy and Allie would enjoy that."

He scrolled down the page. "They're certainly bringing in a lot of singing and dancing groups. There are performances every hour."

I read a menu that had been posted. "The food should be fun to try out. I love piroshki. I've never had blini before. It says it's a Russian crepe with different kinds of fillings. I like sampling new dishes." Then I noticed the pickled herring. "Usually," I added.

We did more searching through the ongoing events, the different food courts, and the scheduled activities. The Cossacks were listed twice.

"I want to watch the Cossacks. They're amazing horseback riders. Are you interested in seeing them? They perform at ten and two."

"Sure. Either time works for me," Scott said.

"Let's go at ten. If I enjoy them, I could see the second performance at two."

"A deal and a date." He stood. "Now, it's time for pie. It should be cool enough."

A date? I'd just made plans to meet Scott and watch an event together. Yep. It fit the definition of a date.

He smiled. "Get ready to taste the first pie you've ever made."

I could tell he was trying to let go of his upset. The smile he gave me wasn't the lighthearted one he'd worn earlier, but it was a step in the right direction. However, I didn't think we'd get back to our merry mood of earlier today.

"Let's get to the best part of cooking: eating." He took two small plates from the cupboard and handed me a knife and a pie server.

I took them. "I've cut Mom's pies before. I should be able to handle this."

"Remember, you need enough for all the Sentinels…unless you want to make another pie." He cocked an eyebrow at me.

I rolled my eyes at him in response, then traced lines on the pie to make eight pieces. I could give one to Helen…that was, if it tasted good.

I cut two pieces and placed them on the plates. Scott went to the refrigerator and pulled out a container of ice cream and grabbed a scoop from a drawer. He added French vanilla to each plate and returned the carton to the freezer.

The grin he gave me this time looked tired but genuine. "Congratulations on baking your first pie." He filled his fork.

"Thanks." I took a bite and relished the sweet taste of the apple mixture with a hint of cinnamon…and the crust was flaky!

"I'd say your first effort was a great success," Scott said as he took another bite.

"It's delicious. Without your guidance, I know it wouldn't have turned out like this." I put my fork down. "Thank you. I had a lot of fun."

"I did, too."

A shadow crossed his face, and I suspected the thought of our murder investigation had flitted across his mind.

"You can store it at room temperature for a couple of days. I have a container the pie fits in. I don't need it back right away." A twinkle returned to his blue eyes. "You're welcome to use it for your next pie."

"I don't know when that's going to be," I replied. "I'm sure I'll get it back to you before that happens."

He went to get the container, and I put our dishes in the sink.

We walked together as he carried the pie out to my Jeep. The wind had picked up, bringing wisps of fog with it.

He put the pie on the floor behind the seat. "I'll see you Saturday at ten."

"Thanks again for the wonderful lesson…and your incredible patience."

"You're welcome. Do you have any idea what you want to work on next?"

I laughed. "Not right now. I need to get some of the flour out of my hair before I start contemplating lesson three." I got in my vehicle. "See you this weekend."

"Great." He turned and entered the community center.

I drove down the road.

A deal and a date, he'd said.

A date.

That was the first time the word had come up in our relationship. I mulled it over. It wasn't a romantic get-together. It was just meeting a friend at an event. It didn't really have any significance. Or did it? I'd been the one to suggest it. Maybe I was finally beginning to heal…and trust again.

My ex-husband had cheated on me. The fact that it was with my best friend had ratcheted up the hurt a notch. The pain seared deep into my heart and my psyche. Scott had been open and honest with me. He didn't strike me in the least as someone who would deceive me.

What other than love made for a good relationship? The first word that came to mind was *trust*, followed by being able to follow my own path. Accepting me as I was. Being able to communicate with each other was next. Scott let me know how he felt but didn't push for change.

I reached Redwood Cove Bed and Breakfast and was happy to have my mental meanderings come to an end for now.

As I finished parking, my cell phone rang. Rudy. I hoped it wasn't more bad news.

"Kelly, the police called and said a man has come in claiming the dagger is his. Someone had stolen the knife from him. They want me to come in to see if he's my half brother." Excitement stirred in his voice.

"Rudy, great news." Then I paused. I was concerned about him getting his hopes up. "But what if he's not?"

"I haven't found him in all this time, so it would mean life continuing on the same." Worry crept into his voice. "If it's not him, what will the police do if the person insists the dagger is his?"

"The police will have to decide how to proceed. Let's take it one step at a time." I looked at my watch. "I can be at your place in about ten minutes if you want to go now."

"We'll be waiting."

Rather than go inside, I called the inn from my Jeep, and Helen answered. "Hi. Rudy and Ivan need my help again. I don't know if I'll make it back in time to help with the wine and appetizers."

"No problem, Kelly. I've got it covered. Tommy and I can eat over here again if you don't make it back by dinnertime."

"Thanks, Helen."

I started the Jeep up and headed for the brothers' home. What if, after all these years, Rudy was reunited with his sister and brother? Then I thought of Ivan. Where did he fit into the relationship? Rudy said he hadn't been allowed to attend school with them. Had they spent time together? Were they friends?

Now it was my turn to stop questioning or worrying and let the story unfold.

The brothers were outside waiting. They got in, and we proceeded to the police station.

"I can't imagine I'd recognize him after all these years," Rudy said. "But I can ask him questions that will reveal whether he's my brother or not."

"Yah," Ivan said. "Can ask in Russian, too."

Rudy nodded. "True, but if he's not spoken it since he was a child, that wouldn't be fair. I have enough memories of things we did together. I'll know if it's him or not."

We checked in at the front desk, then were escorted to Deputy Stanton's office. We entered, and Rudy came to a sudden stop. An elderly man with a striking resemblance to him sat across from Stanton.

Rudy stared. "Timur? Is that you?"

"Rudolph?" The man rose slowly. Tears filled his eyes. "Rudolph? Can it be?"

They hugged. Both were now crying.

"Rudolph. I can't believe it."

After all the years of searching, Rudy had finally found Timur.

Chapter 12

Timur turned to Ivan. "This must be your half brother Ivan." He extended his hand.

Ivan blinked rapidly a couple of times, and Rudy frowned slightly. They always called each other *brother.* There'd never been a distinction made that they weren't full brothers.

Ivan and Timur shook hands.

A younger blond man who'd been sitting off to the side came forward. "I'm Clay Johnson, Timur's nephew."

Clay Johnson, the man whose name was on the dead man's ledger for selling coins like Rudy's. I wondered what kind of relationship he had with the gold dealer.

I stuck out my hand. "I'm Kelly Jackson, manager of Redwood Cove Bed and Breakfast and a friend of Rudy and Ivan. Pleased to meet you."

Timur shook my hand, as did Clay.

"Gentlemen," Deputy Sheriff Stanton addressed them. "It's wonderful you've been reunited. I'm sure you have a lot to catch up on. Right now, I'd like to settle the ownership of this dagger." He pointed to the knife on his desk.

"As I told you, sir, that is mine, and it was stolen." Timur looked at Rudy. "Do you still have your dagger?"

"Yes. What about our sister, Verushka? Does she have hers? Are you in contact with her?"

"She still has hers as well," Timur replied. "We live together."

"It's all well and good you two feel like you recognize each other," Stanton said, "but I need more verification than that. Rudy told us your ages when you last saw each other and how many years it's been since then."

Rudy nodded. "I understand. There are many questions I can ask that only Timur would know the answers to." He gave a sheepish smile. "There were a few scrapes we got into we never told anybody about."

Rudy asked a question in Russian, and Timur responded in kind. About ten minutes of rapid-fire exchanges took place. I actually thought I saw Rudy blush at one point. It ended with both men laughing heartily, standing up, and slapping each other on the back.

Rudy looked at Stanton. "This is Timur, my half brother. That is his knife, or his sister's."

"If you need to see the other knife, it can be arranged," Timur said. "And my sister can come in as well."

"That won't be necessary," Stanton said. "I'm convinced."

Timur looked at Rudy and Ivan. "You must come for a visit. We live a little over an hour north of here. Tomorrow. Lunch. Noon. Will that work? We have much to catch up on. And bring your friend, Ms. Jackson."

Rudy looked at Stanton. "Is that okay, Deputy Stanton? I know you asked me to stay in the area."

"That's fine. It's close enough." Stanton stood, picked up the knife, walked around his desk, and handed it to Timur.

Timur took it. "It is a true joy to have it back. I value it greatly as a family heirloom. Thank you, Deputy Stanton."

"You're welcome. I'm glad we were able to return it to its rightful owner," Stanton said. "There's still the business of who stole it to figure out, though."

"I reported the theft to our local authorities," Timur said. "They questioned some men we had working on the property but didn't learn anything."

Timur put the dagger on the seat of his chair. He pulled a box from a briefcase on the floor next to him. After opening it, he took out a sheath matching the one that housed Rudy's knife. He slid his dagger into its case, placed it in the box, and put the container back where he'd gotten it.

"I'd like to ask Clay a few questions in private about another matter," Deputy Stanton said.

We took our cue to leave and departed the office. The reception area had a half dozen chairs and vending machines. Rudy and Timur sat next to each other and talked a blue streak in Russian. I leafed through a magazine, and Ivan checked out the food choices. Clay joined us after a short wait.

"Everything okay?" Timur asked Clay.

He nodded. "I'll tell you outside."

We went to the parking lot. Clay and Timur stopped at an older black Mercedes sedan.

Clay took keys out of his pocket. "The policeman questioned me about Alexander Koskov, the gold merchant who was murdered. I'd sold him some coins, and my name was in his ledger."

It sounded like he was in the same situation as Rudy, selling coins as money was needed.

"Did you know him well?" I asked.

"No. I did business with him a couple of times. That's it." He turned to Rudy and Ivan. "Do you have an email address? If so, I'll send you detailed directions on how to get to our home."

Rudy gave him the information.

Timur hugged Rudy again. "Tomorrow, then."

The two men climbed into the Mercedes, and they drove off.

"Kelly, do you want to go to the lunch?" Rudy asked. "If not, we can look into someone else driving us. We've hired people to help us before."

"I'd enjoy seeing more of the area. I'm happy to drive you."

And maybe I'd learn more about Clay's relationship with the gold dealer and how the knife made it from their place to the fishing boat.

I drove the brothers home and made plans to pick them up at ten thirty. I returned to the inn and took the pie out of the Jeep, entered the kitchen, and put it on the counter. Helen was adding cheese to one of the guest trays.

"Hi, Kelly. Where did the pie come from? It looks beautiful."

"Uh…I made it."

I had joked with Helen numerous times about my lack of cooking skills.

Helen's eyes widened. "You made it?"

"Yes, with lots of help from Scott."

Helen knew I had agreed to take lessons from Scott. I went on to share with her the events of the afternoon, including Scott's distinguished Silver Sentinel appearance.

"There's a slice of pie there for you," I added.

"Thanks, Kelly. I'll share it with Tommy tonight."

"I'll take care of the wine and appetizers," I said. "and I'll wash the dishes. You've done more than your fair share the last couple of days, and I'm sure Tommy is ready for dinner."

"Thanks, Kelly. His high-energy level makes him an eating machine."

I finished in the kitchen and checked on the fire in the parlor. The flames danced and an occasional spark flew into the air. It was burning well. Back in my rooms, I took out the container of mac and cheese I'd left to thaw in the refrigerator from my first lesson with Scott and put it in the microwave.

That recipe had been a lot easier than today's pie, but we were talking gourmet Scott, so we'd used four cheeses—sharp cheddar, Gruyère, Asiago, and Fontina. I had learned that panko breadcrumbs, the topping we used, were a Japanese style of crumbs. On the ranch, we used commercial-size containers of regular breadcrumbs.

Mom was a great cook. Her priorities for meals were healthy, tasty, filling, and plenty of it. When you were feeding a crew of hungry cowboys and a growing family, there wasn't time for fancy. Grandpa, Dad, my sister and her husband, my two brothers, and now my sister's twin babies all still lived on the ranch.

I was the only one who had left. I loved my family and the ranch, but I'd always had an independent streak. Sometimes that was a good thing, sometimes not. It had pushed me to see more of the world and find a place that felt like my own niche...which I had here in Redwood Cove. I was grateful for that.

I ate the last bite of my dinner and reflected on the day. I was glad Scott had seemed to come to terms about the murder we were investigating. After rinsing my dishes, I made a last check of the parlor. Mere embers remained of the fire. I called it a night.

* * * *

In the morning, Helen and I did the breakfast baskets as usual, and I caught her up on the latest events. When we were finished delivering the food, I sat at the counter, looking over some food orders.

Helen pulled baklava out of the refrigerator. "Kelly, I need to take this to a meeting of the Russian Heritage group. Some of them are getting together with the ground crew and the performers to talk about a few last-minute details. I'll pick up the baskets when I get back."

"I've been wanting to see where the event is taking place. I'd be happy to take it for you."

"Wonderful! With a full house, breakfast cleanup has been keeping me extra busy."

I hoped Vladimir would be there. This would be the perfect opportunity to talk to him.

My Redwood Cove Bed and Breakfast fleece hung on a hook at the back door, and I put it on and picked up the baklava. When I reached my

Jeep, I placed the tray behind the driver's seat and followed the directions Helen had given me.

The field being used by the festival was on the outskirts of town and several large structures occupied it. I'd read in a tourist brochure one barnlike structure housed several conference rooms and had a large open area. That was where the meeting was being held.

I carried the pastry in and saw that chairs had been set up in the main area. People milled around, some in costume. A musical group with stringed instruments practiced in one corner, the melody sounding plaintive and sad.

Vladimir was there. He'd chosen more casual dress today and wore tan cotton slacks and a dark blue sweater over a white shirt. Not so Alena, who I saw talking with two women in colorful skirts, wearing white, puffy-sleeved blouses and scarves over their heads. Alena wore a tailored black jacket with matching slacks.

Vladimir saw me and walked over. "Ahh…more of the delicious baklava. It can go over there with the refreshments." He pointed to a table off to the side, which held coffee and water. "I apologize for not returning your phone call as yet. My schedule's been uncertain, and I've been waiting until I had a better idea of when we could meet. I planned on contacting you today."

We headed for the table.

"My plans have been in flux as well," I said. "Delivering the baklava has given me the chance to see the festival area, something I've been wanting to do."

I put the sweets next to where plates and forks had been set out, then asked the questions I'd prepared. They didn't take long.

Vladimir stepped away and addressed the group. "Please help yourself to refreshments…and the baklava has arrived. We'll start the meeting shortly."

People quickly moved toward the table, and I joined Vladimir off to one side to escape the growing crowd.

"Thank you for the information about the event." Now came the hard part—asking questions about the dead man. I wasn't with the police, and I wondered how Vladimir would react.

A man with a shaved head, wearing a T-shirt marked CREW, came over. "Where do you want the podium?" he asked Vladimir, giving me a few minutes to think.

Vladimir spoke with him briefly and returned to my side. "I'm sorry for the interruption, Ms. Jackson."

"No problem, and please call me Kelly."

"And I, as you know, am Vladimir."

We exchanged smiles, then I dove in. "You knew Alexander Koskov. Did you hear he was murdered?"

He nodded. "Yes, I heard. The police questioned me, and some of the other committee members. Terrible turn of events. I met him some time ago in San Francisco. We did some business together and saw each other at various Russian functions."

"He hasn't been in the area long. His body was found on my friend's boat. The police questioned him about whether or not Koskov had any enemies. He wasn't aware of any. Do you know if he had any problems in San Francisco?"

He shook his head. "Not that I know of. But then, we weren't close."

Vladimir glanced at the front of the room. Alena was there, and she waved at me. I waved at her in return. She then gave Vladimir a come hither gesture with her hand.

He turned to me. "I've got to help. Please call me if you have any more questions."

He left. Not much there, other than that they'd done some business together and knew each other socially. Alexander had come on pretty strong with *my good friend* at the meeting. It seemed as if he felt a stronger connection to Vladimir than I'd just heard.

I returned to the inn. Helen was beginning to prepare the pastries for tomorrow. From the sweet smell of freshly squeezed oranges, I guessed we were having orange nut muffins. They were among my favorites...but then, I liked everything Helen baked.

A familiar rattle in the driveway announced the arrival of Daniel Stevens in his beloved blue vintage Volkswagen bus. He was a single dad and devoted to his daughter, Allie. Her Native American heritage had given her ebony hair that fell to her waist. He had started at Redwood Cove Bed and Breakfast as a handyman and was part of the inn's family, so to speak. Helen, Tommy, Daniel, Allie, and I often gathered together on Sunday night to share dinner and a movie.

I watched as he got out of his vehicle. He opened the side door, bending over his tall frame, his black ponytail swinging to the side. Then he straightened up with a large paper bag in one arm, closed the vehicle, and walked up the back porch.

I waved and opened the door for him. "Hi, Daniel. Looks like you have a delivery."

"The fresh produce that didn't make it yesterday arrived, along with profuse apologies for the mix-up."

We had decided to share duties and had consolidated our orders. We each had areas we were in charge of. It saved us time and allowed for better pricing.

As we unpacked, I caught him up on what was happening. He'd been in the area a long time, and another pair of eyes and ears was always helpful.

I folded the empty paper bag. "Do you know Rick Stapleton?"

"I do. Nice enough guy. He helps me from time to time. He isn't interested in hard work or being on a schedule for any length of time. He floats from job to job."

"Do you know where he lives?"

"No. That changes pretty regularly as well. Why do you ask?"

"He was fired by Alexander Koskov, the murdered man. The Sentinels and I are looking into his death because of the connection to Rudy and Ivan."

"That's not the first time he's lost a job," Daniel said.

"Would you be willing to talk to him to see what you can learn?"

"Sure. I have some easy odds and ends to be done around Ridley House. I can have a conversation with him while we work."

"If possible, I'd like to meet him, get my own sense of what he's like."

Daniel thought for a moment. "You and I have talked about stabilizing the inn's sign in the front yard. I can bring him over to help with that."

"Thanks. I'd appreciate it."

Daniel took off, and I went to change for lunch, figuring slacks were more appropriate than my usual blue jeans. Stapleton didn't sound like someone angry enough to kill Koskov over losing his job. Maybe he had other reasons for killing Alexander. Did they have an argument? Had he gotten caught stealing? Someone had gone to a lot of trouble to put in the second set of surveillance cameras. Who had them installed? Who were they watching?

Chapter 13

Daniel texted to say he'd reached Rick, and they would be working together that day. He'd bring him over a little before four. I replied that would be fine. If I had to miss a few minutes of the Silver Sentinels' meeting, it wasn't a problem.

It was time to pick up the brothers. I drove to their place and parked. Before I could get out of the Jeep and knock on the door, Ivan and Rudy came out, Ivan sporting a black Russian fisherman's hat I knew he put on for special occasions. He wore a heavy cream-colored cable-knit sweater and black trousers. Rudy had opted for tan pants and a navy sweater vest over a green-and-navy-plaid shirt.

They piled in, and we were off. Rudy had emailed me the directions Clay had sent, and I'd checked a map for clarification. I hadn't been as far north as we were traveling today. As soon as we were out of Fort Peter, the scenery began to change. The coast was no longer visible as we wound up barren mountains. A steep drop into an unforgiving gulch below bordered us on the left as we drove up the narrow road.

I'd driven curvy roads before, but none of them had matched the number of turns and the steepness of this one. We stopped at a blinking red light on a cart. A landslide had closed one lane and cars were forced to take turns around it in single file. The last car of the line going downhill passed us and our light turned green.

A few more turns and the road began to head out toward the ocean. Soon we were in view of the crashing waves and craggy rocks. Redwood trees began to appear. It wasn't long before we had towering trees on both sides, with the Pacific Ocean peeking through at intervals.

I checked the odometer and knew we were close. A small sign with Russian lettering appeared, and I turned in as I'd been instructed. We drove on a gravel road deep into the redwood forest. Suddenly, we entered a clearing with a massive structure in front of us with turrets and bright green onion-shaped domes sprouting from light red stone towers. Several smaller buildings dotted the property.

Rudy and Ivan gasped in unison.

"It's the Russian mansion," Rudy said.

Ivan nodded. "Yah."

I stopped the car and gazed at the colorful buildings. "What do you mean?"

"It looks exactly like the one the prince and his family lived in while in Russia."

"Wow! It's beautiful." I continued driving toward the front of the largest structure; I found it hard to think of it as a house. There was a parking area off to the side. I pulled in and we got out.

Timur had come out onto the expansive front porch to greet us. "Welcome. You made it. Come. Everything is ready."

We walked up the porch's wide steps and followed him through the front door.

Rudy and Ivan gasped again.

"Timur, this is the home from Russia. How can that be?"

"It is a story I will tell you. Let's join Verushka and Clay in the dining room. We will talk over lunch."

We entered a formal dining room with a long wooden table and high-backed chairs. A tall, stately woman dressed in a long black dress, her braided hair coiled around on top of her head, approached us. Clay waved at us from where he sat.

The woman gave Rudy a hug. "Rudy, my brother, I never thought this day would come."

"Neither did I, Verushka." Rudy took her hand and held it for a moment. "Neither did I."

"And, Ivan, so good you are here with us." Verushka didn't hug him but gave his arm a slight squeeze.

She approached me. "I'm Verushka Johnson. I'm so glad you could join us today."

"Kelly Jackson. Thank you for the invitation."

Verushka pointed to where we were to sit. I was seated between Clay and Ivan. Rudy had Verushka and Timur on either side of him across from us. A middle-aged woman in a maid's uniform of black blouse and skirt, wearing a white ruffled cap, filled our water glasses and asked if we wanted tea or coffee.

Ivan joined into a conversation about their childhood reminisces. Everyone spoke in English, I suspected as a polite choice for me…though maybe Clay wasn't fluent in Russian either.

I gazed around the room. Portraits hung on the walls, as well as tapestries similar to ones in Rudy and Ivan's basement. It was a far cry from the Wyoming ranch house I'd grown up in.

I turned to Clay. "This is amazing."

"I grew up in it, so it's what I'm used to," he said. "However, there are times, especially early in the morning, when I feel like I'm transported to another era. It becomes fresh and new to me."

The maid returned with bowls of soup, followed by platters of baked buns I recognized as piroshki.

"Ms. Jackson." Verushka pointed to the individual-size pastries. "These are beef and vegetable piroshki."

"They look delicious…and please, call me Kelly."

Verushka nodded. "As you wish. Please, same for me, first name."

"The soup," Timur said, "is fresh cabbage soup known as shchi, and one of the national dishes of Russia."

The piroshki were passed around, and we began to eat. My soup had a garnish of sour cream and dill weed, making for a pleasing mingling of flavors with the cabbage. I inhaled the healthy, robust aroma and relaxed into its nurturing scent.

"So, the story of the house," Timur said. "Our father and your mother, Tatiana, met up with our grandparents in San Francisco, as planned. We felt there was danger there for us and moved on after we'd done a thorough search, trying to find you. We continued looking for you over the years, but more on that later."

He proceeded to tell us that his grandparents found this property and wanted it to be just like the beloved home they'd left behind. One of the smaller structures I'd seen had been based on the servants' quarters in Russia. It was the first to be built, and the family lived there as their former mansion was recreated.

Local woodworkers had been commissioned to build the furniture. Some of the portraits were originals they'd managed to get out of the country. Others were replicas painted by local artists. Photos enabled the craftsmen and painters to duplicate some of what had been lost.

"We moved into the house in its bare-bones stage, as we heard the workers call it," Verushka added. "It took years to create the rest of what you see."

Timur nodded. "Our grandparents were pleased with the final result. It eased the loss of what they'd known as home in Russia."

"There's so much for us to catch up on," Rudy said. "It's hard to know where to start."

"I agree," Timur said. "But there is one important bit of news that should not wait any longer."

Verushka looked at Rudy and Ivan. "After our grandparents died, our father and your mother were finally married...something they'd wanted to do for a long time."

"Ivan," Timur smiled at him from across the table, "you now have a stepsister and a stepbrother."

"I have a bigger family now," Ivan said, grinning broadly.

"Let's start there," Timur said.

He went to a cabinet and pulled out a document. The maid had cleared the dishes while he'd told his story, and Timur unrolled the parchment paper on the table. It crackled as he spread it out. An intricate tree of names had been artfully drawn.

"This has all the aunts, uncles, cousins, nephews...all the relatives you are now part of."

Clay leaned over toward me. "Would you like to see some of the property?"

"Very much so," I said.

We stood, and Clay said, "I'm going to take Kelly around the house while you talk family."

"Good idea," Verushka said.

"Guys," I said, "we need to leave by two o'clock to be back in time for our meeting."

They nodded and went back to chatting with Timur and Verushka about their extended family. We walked down a wide hallway with decorative stone tile floors. Portraits of relatives gazed at us as we passed by. Clay named a few of them.

While it was all interesting, I wanted to start gathering information. "It's wonderful your uncle got his dagger back."

"I couldn't agree more."

"Do you have any idea how the knife got stolen?"

He shook his head.

"Do you have any idea when it was taken?"

Another headshake. "Not exactly. My uncle hadn't looked at it for about a week."

I was pelting him with questions and decided I'd better give him a reason why. "I love a good mystery, and the dagger on the boat has me intrigued."

Clay smiled. "I can understand why."

Back to the case. "Who was in the house during that time?"

"Only family and servants who have been with us for years."

We entered a library with floor-to-ceiling books. The lit fireplace added some welcome warmth to the cavernous room. I walked to the bookshelves and examined the book titles. Most were in Russian, so I didn't get any idea what the family's reading interests were.

"Did you have any visitors?" I asked as I wandered along the massive collection.

"My sister and her son and daughter came for a couple of days."

I spied some English titles and bent over to read them. They proved to be classics. "What about workmen?" I straightened up.

"We had some outside repair work done to our waterlines, but I never saw any of them near the house."

"Was the house empty at any time?"

"No."

But it's a large house. I bet someone could sneak in and nobody would know it. "How on earth do you think the dagger ended up on the boat?"

Clay shook his head. "No idea. I'm just glad we got it back."

"I'm surprised whoever took it didn't take the sheath."

A slight frown appeared. "My uncle kept the dagger in a drawer next to the bed. The holder was elsewhere. He wanted the knife ready to use if necessary." He pointed to the books I'd been examining. "Those are mine. I majored in English, and taught for a while."

I guessed he was tired of all the questions and ready to talk about something else. There was nothing more for me to ask right now, so I obliged.

"Sorry about all the questions. I read *Nancy Drew* growing up. Where did you teach?"

"At a local high school." He looked at his watch. "We'd better head back. I can show you more on the way."

The same steady eyes of the ancestors followed us on our return.

"Clay, maybe there's something you can help Rudy and Ivan with—the murdered gold dealer. They've been asked not to leave the area. Technically, they're considered suspects until the killer is caught."

"I wondered what was going on when Rudy asked the officer for permission to come here."

"I'm working with Rudy, Ivan, and a group of our friends to find out something that might be helpful for the police in their investigation. Is there anything you can tell me about Alexander? He was new to the area and people know very little about him."

"Not really. I only did business with him a couple of times." He thought for a moment. "He wasn't a gossiper, which I appreciated. I wanted to keep as low a profile with the gold as possible."

"Rudy feels the same. He sells the coins when he needs money for expenses."

"Same here."

"How did you find out about Koskov?" I asked.

"He put an ad in the local paper."

"Who were you using before?"

"Harvey Goldstein."

The gold merchant had lost two customers. It was a niche business I suspected had a very limited clientele. Did he kill Alexander to be sure he wouldn't lose any more people?

And the dagger.

I had wondered if it might be a warning.

Did the fact that Ivan was now officially part of the family have anything to do with the knife's appearance covered with a substance resembling blood? Was a relative concerned he might have an inheritance coming? Money was at the root of many murders. We'd mostly been worried about Rudy. Was it possible Ivan was more of a target?

Chapter 14

We made a circuit of part of the house. I viewed a parlor, a second much-smaller dining room, and a sitting room overlooking lush gardens filled with a variety of flowers. The windows were closed, but I could imagine the intermingling of sweet floral scents.

We talked while we walked. Clay had been an English teacher in the nearby town of Greenville. He'd been married for a short while. A divorce ended the marriage. The remote area wasn't for everyone. When his father, who'd been living on the estate, died, he'd moved back into the house to help care for it and his aging relatives.

We joined the others.

"Thank you for the tour. I really enjoyed it. It's a magnificent estate."

"You're welcome. If you come again, I'll show you the grounds."

"Speaking of coming again," Timur said, "Rudy and Ivan, you inherited a number of items. We will gather them together as soon as possible and contact you when we have all of them."

"Rudy," Clay said, "I heard so much about the case and the three daggers growing up, I'd love to see them all together. Would you be willing to bring it and your knife when you come back?"

Rudy nodded. "I agree it would be nice to see them together. Yes, I'll bring them."

Verushka picked up a delicate-looking teacup and took a sip. "It has been a long time since I've done a formal tea service. When you come for your belongings, I will serve you a special tea."

"That would be wonderful," Rudy said. "It has been many years since I've seen one. I remember us watching from a distance and then pretending to do a tea service on our own in our kitchen."

Rudy and Ivan rose.

"Wait," Timur said. "Before you go, I have something to show you."

He left and came back a couple of minutes later holding a photograph. Timur put it on the table, where we could all see it. I recognized the man and woman from the picture I'd seen at the brothers' home. The prince was in full regalia, rows of medals on his chest, boots up to his knees. Their mother wore a long white dress, a bouquet of roses in her hands. The love in their expressions flowed out of the photo, giving it a life of its own.

Rudy stared at it with a slight smile and sadness in his eyes. "I'm so happy they married. At least one positive thing happened from the upheaval of leaving Russia."

"Wish I could've seen Mother again," Ivan said. "So glad to see picture and her joy. Good to know."

"They were happy together for many years," Verushka said. "Their only sadness was not finding the two of you."

"Our father died of a heart attack," Verushka said. "Your mother died not long after. People say you can't die of a broken heart, but I'm not so sure in her case."

Ivan let out a long sigh.

"Next time, we'll tell you more about our journey and our lives," Timur said.

We bid them good-bye and started the drive back on the treacherous road. I understood now why they hadn't found each other: the extreme isolation, the lack of communication when they'd arrived in America, and their sense of being unwelcome. They'd built their piece of Russia, and that was where they'd lived.

The brothers talked among themselves about all the newfound family they'd discovered. They'd gone from the two of them to a slew of relatives. They seemed excited about it. I suspected there'd be opportunities for some fun family gatherings ahead. It was wonderful to see their smiles and happiness replace the frowns and fear they'd been experiencing the last couple of days.

The trip hadn't netted much in terms of solving the murder or the question of who had stolen the dagger. The coin dealer had lost at least two clients, and there was an explanation as to why the knife and the sheath weren't together. That was it. I stopped thinking about it and concentrated on my driving as I'd reached the dangerous, curving part of the road.

As we got closer to town and the road straightened out, I interrupted them. "Daniel is bringing Rick Stapleton, the employee fired by Koskov, to the inn so I can meet him. It's under the guise of needing help with a repair—one Daniel and I were going to do. Daniel is working with him today and hopefully will learn some new information for us."

"Good idea to meet him," Rudy said. "I've heard it said a picture is worth a thousand words. I believe meeting a person speaks volumes about their personality."

I nodded. "That's how I feel."

We arrived at the inn about ten minutes before the Silver Sentinels' meeting was set to start. Daniel's van pulled in beside us. A man occupied the passenger seat.

"Please tell the others to start if I'm not there by four o'clock. I'll catch up when I get there."

Ivan and Rudy nodded and went in.

"Hi, Kelly." Daniel got out of the van. "I'd like you to meet Rick Stapleton. He's going to help me fix the wobbly sign."

A skinny man in a tattered denim shirt and blue jeans came around the front of the vehicle. His brown hair had begun to recede, exposing pale, white skin.

"Nice to meet you," I said. "I'm glad you were available to help Daniel."

"Kelly Jackson is the manager of Redwood Cove Bed and Breakfast," Daniel said.

"Hi there." He turned to Daniel, "Hey, Dan my man, where do you want these?" He gestured with the toolbox he was carrying.

Dan my man?

Somehow that didn't fit with the Daniel I knew: a proud, reserved Native American.

"We're going to be working on the sign in the front yard. Go ahead, and I'll meet you there."

"Sure thing." He ambled off.

When Rick was out of earshot, I asked, "How did it go? Did you find out anything?"

"Quite a bit. The sign won't take us long. I'll drive him back to his car and then join you and the Sentinels."

"Okay. I'll let them know."

Daniel left to fix the sign, and I went into the building.

The rest of the group was already there, and Helen had put out drinks as well as dishes for the surprise pie I was about to serve. I noticed a plate of brownies.

"Mary, are these the same kind as the ones you made the other day?" Rudy asked.

She nodded enthusiastically. "They were so tasty. You all seemed to enjoy them so much, I decided to make them again."

"Good choice. They were delicious," I said, and looked around for Mary's extended family, Princess the Chihuahua.

"Where's your four-legged kid?"

"My sister's visiting, so I left Princess there so she could play with her dog. She likes bossing him around."

I placed a brownie on a plate and put it on the table near where I planned to sit. They were still warm, and the delicious sweet smell of chocolate filled the air.

Mary turned to Rudy and Ivan. "Oh," she said breathlessly, "you found your family. How exciting! I can't wait to hear. Thanks for letting us know yesterday after your visit to the police station."

It was clear the communication lines between the group's members were still operating at top speed.

"Yes. What a wonderful event," the Professor said.

"I want to hear, too," Gertie said, "but I feel getting the murder solved takes precedent."

They all nodded.

"I have something to add to the refreshments," I said. "Why don't you take a few minutes to chat while I get it."

They didn't need a second suggestion. The group began pelting the brothers with questions while I retrieved the pie and a server. When I walked in the room, the group looked up and became silent. They knew about my legendary lack of cooking skills and my plans to take lessons from Scott.

I put the pie down next to the plates. "In case you're wondering, I made it. It's safe to eat because Scott was there every step of the way."

"I'm sure it's marvelous, my dear," the Professor said.

I cut everyone a slice and passed out the pieces, along with forks and napkins.

The Professor was the first to comment. "Delicious, Kelly."

Ivan's plate was already clean. "Yah. Good."

"So, this is your second lesson with Scott." Mary put down her fork. Her big grin made her dimples pop into view. "Do you have another one planned?"

I knew all five of them would dearly love to see me in a relationship with Scott. They adored him and, though they'd never said anything directly, there'd been enough hints and suggestions for me to know matchmaking was on their minds.

"No more lessons on the calendar at the moment. I need to recover from this one, and be sure I've gotten all the flour out of my hair and off my clothes."

They laughed, and then Gertie said, "Time to get down to business."

"We now know," the Professor said, "there was no blood on the knife. That changes the scenario completely."

Rudy had picked up the pen to update the charts and became the recorder. He crossed out *blood?* on the dagger chart and added *fake blood.* Under that, he put *owned by half brother Timur.*

"I learned from Clay, Timur's nephew, that there was about a week during which the knife could've been taken," I said. "He told me, to the best of his knowledge, no one but family, including his sister and her son and daughter, and two longtime, trusted employees, had been in the house over that period of time."

Rudy added the information. "The house is a replica of the one in Russia. It's enormous, and there are many ways in and out of it, some of them secret. I know about them because I used some of them. It's possible someone could get in unseen."

"I agree with you," I said. "My tour with Clay wasn't extensive, but it was enough for me to think the same thing."

"If someone stole the dagger to make money with it, why did it end up on the boat?" Gertie asked.

We all shook our heads.

"Maybe someone was on the boat with it, got frightened off, and left it behind," Mary suggested.

"I don't think so," the Professor said, "It would be easy to grab the dagger and run."

This time we all nodded.

"Let's suppose for a moment it's symbolic," the Professor said. "It was stolen by someone not interested in the money they could make selling it. Where does that take us?"

"Could it be some implied threat to Rudy or Ivan?" Gertie asked. "The dagger was out of its sheath and had what appeared to be blood on it."

"I was thinking along those same lines," I said.

Rudy added it to the chart.

I frowned. "The family was the most likely to have access to it. And maybe the message they wanted to send was more important than its worth. They said they didn't know Rudy and Ivan's whereabouts, but we don't know if that's true."

"We found out today our mother married the prince," Rudy said. "That makes Ivan a stepbrother to Timur and Verushka. Perhaps there's an inheritance issue involved."

"Clay, the sister, and her family—any of them could've taken the knife to the boat. Verushka and Timur could have hired someone to drive them, maybe even one of their trusted employees," I added.

Rudy had been writing their names on the dagger chart. Now he added *threat* with a question mark.

"It's an odd case, for sure," Mary said.

We all agreed with her.

"Since there's no explicit threat at this time, I suggest we move on to Alexander Koskov's murder," the Professor said.

Gertie nodded. "Mary and I had an interesting conversation with Harvey Goldstein's mother. His business has been struggling since Alexander opened his shop. She hopes with him gone, her son can get his life back on course again."

I nodded. "Clay told me he used to go to him but switched, like Rudy did."

"Certainly a motive there," the Professor said.

Mary picked up one of her brownies. "Why kill him on their boat?"

"Maybe he pretended to be Rudy and lured him there. It's an out-of-the-way spot," the Professor said.

"It would be easy enough for him to say he had some coins he wanted Alexander to look at and would rather not bring them all into his shop," Gertie added.

"Wouldn't he know it wasn't Rudy's voice?" Mary asked.

I thought for a moment. "Not necessarily. Rudy doesn't usually have an accent. Harvey could've coughed and said he had a bad cold. If he was using a cell phone, the reception usually isn't very good in Fort Peter."

"What about his phone number being seen?" Gertie asked.

"There are ways to block your number," the Professor said. "There's also the pay phone at the market."

Gertie sat up straight. "Okay. We have a motive and possibly how he got Alexander there. Next step?"

"Rudy, I have an idea," I said. "I'd like you to let me take one of your gold coins to Goldstein's shop to sell it…one he wouldn't recognize as yours and isn't one of your really valuable ones. I'm new to the area, so he doesn't know me. It'll give me a chance to meet him, and maybe I can get a reaction when he gives me a price and I tell him Alexander Koskov offered me more than that."

"Excellent idea, Kelly, if Rudy is comfortable with it," the Professor said.

Rudy nodded. "Yes. I am happy to do this. I know just the coin I can give you."

Clay's name was on Alexander's chart from when he was the unknown coin seller on Koskov's ledger. Rudy put *relative* next to Clay's name.

Tom Brodsky's name was underlined as a suspect. Rudy pointed to it. "Do we know anything more about him?"

Negative shakes all around.

"What does he do for a living?" I asked.

"He's an accountant." Gertie frowned. "He's also a docent at Fort Nelsen and has his office there."

"I'll combine a trip to the gold shop and the fort to see what I can learn," I volunteered.

"Professor, what did you find out from your friend who owns the building where Koskov had his shop?" Rudy asked.

"As I texted, he told me it was leased by a company in San Francisco called the Williams Corporation. Alexander was their employee. I located it on the Internet, but the site had very little information. It's a real estate business, leasing and selling."

"You texted us there were two types of surveillance cameras installed. Can you tell us more about them?" I asked.

"Yes. The police asked my friend about them. He'd given permission for their installation. One set was obvious and had notices of their existence. The others were hidden. Those seemed more aimed at watching Alexander."

"Whoa! It sounds like his employers might not have trusted him," Mary said.

"I agree it seems that way," the Professor said. "My friend contacted the company on the lease, and they said they'd send someone up to clear the building. He was fine with that because the rent was paid in advance."

"San Francisco and business." I took out Vladimir's card. "This says he's president of Golden Enterprises, and it's an investment company."

The Professor wrote it down. "I'll check it out and see if I can find any connection to the company on the lease."

"The other person from the San Francisco area is Alena," I said. "I don't know what kind of business she's in. I'll check the information I have on the form she filled out to rent the conference room. Let's put her on Alexander's chart."

Rudy had added the information provided by the Professor and now wrote Alena's name.

"Honey," Mary said, "if you'll email that to me, I'll do the research. You've already got a lot to do."

"Deal," I said.

I looked at the charts. There was only one name that showed up on both—Clay Johnson.

Had he stolen the knife? If so, why leave it on the boat?

Alexander had given him good prices for his gold. What reason would he have to kill him?

I felt like I was going down a dark tunnel with no bright light at the end.

Chapter 15

There was a knock on the door, it opened, and Daniel walked in. "Hi, everybody. I've got some news for you about Rick Stapleton."

"Great, Daniel. Wonderful to have you join us," the Professor said.

"Honey, help yourself to some brownies," Mary chimed in.

"Don't mind if I do. It's been a long day, and chocolate and coffee will perk me up."

Daniel put a couple of treats on a plate, poured himself a cup of the dark French roast we served, and sat next to Mary.

"What did you find out from Rick?" Gertie asked.

Daniel sipped his coffee. "I certainly had no trouble finding out why he was fired. He couldn't tell me enough about what a pain Alexander was."

Rudy started a new sheet of paper with Rick Stapleton's name at the top. "Ready when you are, Daniel."

"Apparently, Alexander had a short fuse and lost his temper on a regular basis. Rick had been the recipient on several occasions when he hadn't put something back in exactly the right place."

"What did Rick do at the store?" Mary asked.

"Waited on customers for the routine purchases. Rick dusted and straightened the place up. Alexander handled all the museum-quality pieces as well as the coins."

Rudy made notes as Daniel talked.

"He unpacked shipments—but not all of them. Some Alexander did himself, after Rick had left for the day."

The Professor's eyebrows went up. "I wonder what was in the boxes he didn't want Rick to see."

Rudy added *boxes?* to the chart.

"No telling," Daniel said. "I asked Rick if he ever saw anything Alexander had unpacked, but he said no. Wasn't his business, so he didn't go looking. Rick's pretty laid back and didn't care to find out."

"What caused the termination of his job?" the Professor asked.

"Alexander accused him of stealing and fired him." Daniel chuckled. "Rick said he told him he couldn't fire him because he quit."

"Do you think he did steal something? Would he do something like that?" I asked.

Daniel shrugged. "Who knows? He's not a close friend, so I can't vouch for his integrity. The way he bounces from job to job, finances might be a problem for him."

"Thanks, Daniel," I said. "That's helpful."

He stood. "Glad to help...and thanks for the killer brownies. Allie's probably home from school now, so I should get going. I told her I'd pick her up and take her to the Ridley House to help with the appetizers. She likes to do it, and I give her extra money in her allowance for pitching in."

Mary went over to the brownies, wrapped several in a napkin, and handed them to Daniel. "Here. These are for you and Allie."

"Thanks. She'll love them."

Daniel left, and we looked at our charts.

"Not a lot of new information, but some," Mary said. "I think we should underline Rick Stapleton and consider him a suspect."

We all nodded in agreement.

I stared at Vladimir's name and thought about our conversation this morning. "Rudy, please put *friend or acquaintance* with a question mark next to Vladimir's name."

Rudy did as I requested.

I explained to the group, "When I saw Alexander at the committee meeting, he appeared to greet Vladimir as a close friend. When I talked to Vladimir this morning, he implied he didn't know Alexander very well."

The Professor twirled his pen. "Vladimir could be lying. The question then becomes why."

"Or," Mary chimed in, "Alexander could have thought they had a stronger relationship...or maybe he was hopeful it would happen."

I nodded. "Vladimir strikes me as a powerful man. Someone who would be valuable to know. I'll keep my eyes and ears open and see if I can learn more."

"Rudy," Gertie said, "I'd like you to add to our Next Steps chart."

Rudy obliged by going to the paper. Under his name, he put *coin to Kelly*. He listed the visits I planned to make. Rudy added Mary and the Professor's *Internet research* with the appropriate tasks.

"Put *follow up with Mrs. Goldstein* under my name," Gertie said. "We have our organic gardening club gathering tomorrow. Maybe I can learn more."

The Professor looked around the room. "Another meeting tomorrow?"

Everyone agreed, and decided one o'clock would work.

"As we've been doing, if anyone discovers something significant, get it out to the group. The sooner we put this together, the better," Gertie said.

She banged the table with her gavel, declaring an official end to the meeting.

They packed up and left. I gathered the dishes and went to the kitchen. Tommy and Fred were curled up together in a beanbag chair. One of the hound's long ears hung over the top of Tommy's leg and the basset snored gently. Tommy was reading a paperback with a dog on the cover.

As I rinsed the dishes, I heard a car on the gravel driveway. I glanced out the back window just as Deputy Stanton got out. The droopy face of Gus filled the open window in the back of the police vehicle. Stanton let him out, and they both climbed the back porch steps.

I opened the door. "Come on in."

He entered, hat in hand. "Howdy, Ms. Jackson…that is, unless you and the Silver Sentinels have solved the crimes and I can call you Kelly again."

I laughed. "We're not there yet, but we're working on it."

I reached down and petted Gus on the top of his head and ran my hand down one of his silky ears. He gave me a bloodhound grin of thanks. Fred trotted over, and they touched noses. Gus and Fred began to tussle and bumped into Stanton's leg.

Helen came from behind the kitchen divider. "Fred. Gus. Sit!"

Both dogs sat so fast they almost sat on each other.

"Good boys." Helen opened a tin on the counter, pulled out two bone-shaped biscuits, and fed them to the dogs. "The wonder of what dog treats can do," she said to us.

Vigorous tail-wagging ensued.

Tommy had put down his book and clambered onto one of the stools at the counter. "Hi, Deputy Stanton."

"How's it going, Tommy?"

"Fine. School was fun. We had a math contest, and I won."

"Congratulations!" the deputy said. "I'm not surprised, knowing what a whiz you are with mathematics."

Tommy grinned and picked up one of the cookies from the plate his mom had put in front of him.

"I was in the area and stopped by to see if you wanted to watch Gus practice tracking tomorrow after school." Stanton said.

Tommy's eyes widened. "Yes! Cool." He looked at his mother. "Is that okay, Mom?"

She smiled at her son and tousled his blond hair. "Sure."

"Is it still okay for Allie to come?" he asked.

"Of course."

"Cool! I'll go text her." He ran to his backpack, next to where he'd been sitting, and took out his phone.

"I'd love to tag along," I said. "I've never watched a training session for tracking before."

"You're more than welcome to join us. What about you, Helen?" Stanton asked.

"I can't tomorrow," she said. "I have another order to do during my afternoon baking hours. My business is booming with people involved in the Russian Heritage Festival being in town." She laughed. "They do love their baklava. I'll make time to take Tommy to the training and pick him up."

"Do you want me to take Tommy with me?" I asked.

"That would be wonderful," Helen replied.

Stanton turned to me. "I'll email you directions. We'll be working for about an hour."

"Do we need to dress in any special way?"

"Sturdy shoes or hiking boots and whatever you need to keep warm."

"Got it."

"So, have you and the crime-solving seniors discovered anything you think I should know?" Stanton asked.

"Follow me to the conference room and you can look at our charts for yourself."

"Bill," said Helen, and held up a foil-wrapped package, "this is for you. It's baklava, something I'm becoming an expert at preparing, I might add. I'll leave it here on the counter."

"Homemade baklava. That'll be a first for me and explains the distinct smell of honey I noticed when I entered."

"You were aware of it that much?" Helen asked.

"My dad was a beekeeper, and I used to help with the hives. It's a scent I'm very familiar with," Stanton said. "Thanks for the treat, Helen. I'm sure it'll be delicious."

Helen blushed a bit and began rinsing dishes in the sink. Stanton and I went down the hallway to the conference room. He walked around, reading our notes, then stopped at the dagger information.

"You've definitely been busy. I know there's a thief still to catch, but now that we know there's no blood on the knife and it's been returned to its rightful owner, I'm putting my attention on the murder."

"We're doing the same."

Stanton surveyed the charts related to Koskov, the suspects, and our next steps.

He pointed to the sheet of paper with Rick's name on it and gave a rueful smile. "You're ahead of us with this guy. He hasn't answered our calls. We found his job application at Koskov's store and checked the address he'd given, but he's no longer living there. How did you manage to find him and get the information?"

"Daniel knows him. I asked if he'd get together with Rick and question him for us. Daniel hired him to do some work today, and they shot the breeze, so to speak. Rick didn't know it wasn't just idle conversation."

"Does Daniel have any idea where he's staying?"

"No. He mentioned he moves around a lot," I replied.

"He's right there. I've heard Rick refer to himself as a professional houseguest."

"What did he mean by that?"

"When people offer him a place to crash, he helps with the cooking, cleaning, and miscellaneous work that needs to be done around the house."

I tilted my head. "Makes sense. Sort of a way to pay them back."

"Right," Stanton replied. "What's the bit about the boxes?"

I explained what Daniel had told us.

Stanton read the information on Koskov's chart. "How did you find out about the two sets of cameras?"

"The Professor is friends with the owner of the building."

Stanton nodded. "Figures. You all do have a way of collecting information. I suppose that's how you know about the San Francisco company."

"Right. You can see the Professor is going to research that."

"Why are the names Alena Stepanova and Vladimir Yeltsin on the chart?"

"Because they're from San Francisco where the Williams Corporation is located and are on the Russian Heritage Committee, as was Koskov. We wondered if one of them might be involved in the store." I smiled. "We don't have the resources you do, so this is our back-door way of checking into things."

"I'll keep them in mind when we find out about the leasing company."

"I know where they're staying, if you want to get in touch with them," I said.

"Thanks. I have all the information you've gathered, except for Rick. Good to know why he got fired. I'll add it to my notes. And it's interesting about the boxes. I'll add that as well. If you or Daniel see Rick again, tell him to call us."

"Will do."

Stanton frowned. "Better yet, maybe I'll stop by and borrow Daniel's phone to call him. Now that I know Rick's communicated with Daniel, it's pretty clear he's avoiding us."

"We're meeting tomorrow at one. If anything new comes up, I'll let you know."

"Thanks." He adjusted his heavy leather belt. "Well, time to go."

He left, and I took over our normal nightly routine of keeping appetizers and wine out for our guests from Helen. After dinner, I pulled out Alena's conference room form. She listed herself as a self-employed financial planner.

Curious, I did a search for her name on the Internet. I found a professional-looking website with a stunning photo of her in the right-hand corner. It listed the different services she could provide. I went back to the search list to see if there was anything else that jumped out at me.

There was.

A headline read, MAJOR RUSSIAN MAFIA FIGURE, BORIS BARANOV, CONVICTED.

I looked at the article. A photo showed a crowd of people watching a large, heavyset man in handcuffs being escorted out of a courthouse.

Alena was in the crowd.

She held a handkerchief in her hand.

She was crying.

The first sentence of the story said, "Alena Stepanova, daughter of Boris Baranov, was in tears as her father was led away."

Chapter 16

The Russian Mafia? Were they part of what was happening? I sat back in my chair. Just because Alena's father was part of the mob, it didn't mean Alena had anything to do with them. I didn't know much about how the Mafia worked from the few articles I'd read, but some of them mentioned the families of Mafia members were often intentionally kept at a distance from the organized crime activities for their safety.

Still...knowing there was a connection added a new twist to our investigation. Her father could be involved and she might not know it. Being in prison wouldn't keep him from making things happen on the outside.

I sent the information I had to Mary and turned off the computer. Mary would research it. She was thorough, and we'd know more tomorrow. Sleep came fast. It had been a long day.

The next morning, I was up bright and early. Stanton had emailed me directions for the tracking training and said to meet him there at four. I asked Daniel to bring Allie over at three forty-five. Rudy texted he'd be over at eight with the coin. An email from Alena asked if she could meet with me in the afternoon to arrange another committee meeting. I replied that two thirty would work.

Helen and I delivered breakfast baskets, then I placed a few orders and checked on the computer for directions to Goldstein's shop in Fort Peter. I went to the kitchen, where Helen was washing the guests' dishes, and helped put away the morning breakfast paraphernalia.

As I finished, Rudy and Ivan appeared at the back door, and I signaled them in.

"Good morning, you two," I said.

"Hi, Kelly," Rudy said in a decidedly cheerier tone than I had heard for a while.

Ivan nodded vigorously, a wide grin on his face. "Verushka call. Say they almost have all our belongings together. Go Sunday."

"She invited you as well, Kelly," Rudy said.

"I'd love to join you, and I'm happy to drive again."

And that will give me another opportunity to ask questions.

Rudy pulled a pouch from his pocket. "Here is the coin I found for you. I've only sold gold coins before, so it's not like any Harvey has seen from me."

He dropped a shiny silver coin in my hand. I examined it and saw an intricate coat of arms on one side with a crown at the top. On the other side was the number five, words in Russian, and the year 1849.

"It's in mint condition," Rudy said. "I checked current prices and found one for one thousand nine hundred fifty dollars. I have several of them."

"Perfect. It'll be interesting to see how he reacts. I'll let you know at the meeting this afternoon."

We bid each other farewell, and I went to get my down jacket. Fog often lingered nearby and created a special chill all its own. I retrieved my purse and my driving notes and took off in my Jeep. My first visit would be the fort because the turnoff for it was on the way into town.

Signs marked the road to take to the fort, and I followed them through the towering redwoods, which were now part of my life. A large wooden sign indicated I'd arrived at my destination, and I turned into the parking lot. I found a place for the Jeep and got out. I stopped to admire the huge structure in front of me, complete with a wooden fence surrounding it like I'd only seen on television. Logs with pointed ends had been secured together to keep out invaders.

The massive gates were open, and I walked in. A sign directed me to a tourist information desk, another to business offices. I decided to gather some information before seeing if Tom was in.

The helpful volunteer manning the desk gave me a map and a brochure. I leafed through it and saw the fort was built in 1812 and was part of an endeavor of the Russian American Company. Shipbuilding was one of their main goals because of the abundance of timber. The fort was particularly known for having the first windmill in California.

I walked out into the compound's yard, a combination of bare dirt and native grasses. A large fire pit occupied one side. Buildings two stories high dotted various points of the perimeter.

I paused for a moment, reflecting on what life must have been like in those days. After a storm, mud would've replaced the packed dirt. Was the fire pit a communal place for meals? I imagined the challenges of tending the fire and the discomfort of cooking in inclement weather.

It was part of life for the people who lived then. They didn't know the comforts future generations would enjoy. I saluted their strength and brave spirit.

A sign off to my left identified a group of buildings as offices. I walked over to them and found a map on a stand. Tom's office was listed. It looked like an original building, but when I went in, the interior was completely modern. Tom had a corner unit on the second floor. I found it. Black lettering on the door said *come in*, so I entered.

Tom looked up from a cluttered desk. "Ms. Jackson, what a surprise; a pleasant one, I might add."

He hurried around from behind his desk, and we shook hands. Two windows behind him provided an expansive view of the fort's grounds.

I wanted my visit to appear as casual as possible, so I said, "I was on my way to do an errand in Fort Peter and saw the signs for this place. On a whim, I decided to stop by."

"I'm so glad you did." He removed papers from a chair and pulled it in front of his desk. "Please, sit down."

He went back around his desk and sat, and I settled in the seat he'd cleared for me.

I looked over his shoulder. "Your office has a great view."

"Yes. I consider myself very fortunate. A committee oversees the fort. While we hated to convert one of the original buildings into offices, the fort is very expensive to maintain. We kept the outer structure so people could appreciate the whole fort community. The offices are always full and there's a waiting list. The rent is covering all our costs and then some."

"This is a very impressive structure. I can really get a sense of what life must have been like in the eighteen hundreds."

"Have you looked into any of the buildings yet?"

"No. I just got here. I picked up information at the Tourist Center."

"Wait until you see the rooms they lived in, the windows the guards looked through, keeping watch for possible enemies. It's amazing."

Excitement and passion gave his voice a different pitch and a high level of energy.

"I can imagine."

He stood. "Do you have time for a tour?"

"A short one, yes."

"Let's go, then." He grabbed a jacket off his coatrack.

He proceeded to take me around to the different buildings, explaining the purpose of each. Some were for supplies, others for goods to trade. Barracks for the men on guard were part of what he showed me. Bare bones all the way. I was cold in my down parka and these people had had so little.

"I'd better get back to work," Tom said after the tour. "Please feel free to wander around as much as you like. Stop by on your way out so I can say good-bye and answer any questions you might have."

He left, and I went up worn stairs to a lookout post. As I gazed out the window, I had the chills. How many men over a hundred years ago had looked out at the same view, wondering if enemies were going to appear. I spotted a locked cabinet that held a simple-looking, single-barrel rifle. What kind of defense would that have been?

I descended to the living areas. A cot with a couple of blankets and a chipped water pitcher and a bowl occupied the top of a scarred wooden bedside table. I had to admit I enjoyed living in my era. It was time to leave for my next stop.

I went to Tom's office and sat in the chair while he finished a phone call.

He hung up. "How did you enjoy your visit?"

"Fantastic. It was somewhat unnerving to stand where people stood over a hundred years ago and think about what their life was like."

Tom nodded enthusiastically. "I know exactly what you're talking about. Even though I've been through the rooms time after time, I still get the same feeling. It's like, for an instant, I go back in time."

"I can see why you're so passionate about having the festival here."

Tom smiled. "I'm glad to hear that."

"I wonder why Alexander was so set against it?"

At the mention of Alexander's name, Tom's face darkened, and the knuckles on his clenched hands turned white.

He took a deep breath, as if forcing himself to relax. "For his own gain, I assure you. Some of the other committee members are already voicing a desire to have it here next year now that he's gone. I think they were influenced by what appeared to be Alexander's close relationship with Vladimir."

"Why would that matter?" I asked.

"Vladimir was new on the committee this year. He invested a lot of money in this festival and promoted it in San Francisco. Committee members hope he'll do it again and want to stay on his good side."

"Did Vladimir want it in Redwood Cove and not the fort?"

"I never heard him voice a preference. I'm certainly going to make an effort to have him come for a visit before he leaves."

I rose. "Thank you again for your time and the tour. I'm really enjoying learning about the area."

"Any time."

As I drove back to the highway, I thought about the road I was on. After yesterday's drive, I expected a similar treacherous trip based on Alexander's comments. Instead, I found myself dealing with gentle curves, a decently wide road, and the fort was only a short distance from the main highway.

I was inclined to agree with Tom that Alexander's comments were exaggerated, and that he had other reasons for wanting the festival adjacent to Redwood Cove. I felt like I had found a motive for why he might want people to think he was good friends with Vladimir…it influenced others to do what he wanted.

As for Tom, he was passionate about the fort and what it represented. He'd had what appeared to be a visceral reaction when Alexander's name entered the conversation.

Passion had led people to kill.

Had that emotion pushed Tom to murder Alexander?

Chapter 17

Gray.

That was the word that struck me as I sat in my Jeep looking at the coin dealer's shop. After the drive up the road with the constant presence of the Pacific Ocean, the lackluster building before me seemed so lifeless and without color. Gray pavement with trash piled up along the gray curb alongside the gray sidewalk. I couldn't tell if the background of the store's sign was painted gray or just needed washing.

The bold black lettering said GUNS COINS ANTIQUES—BUY AND SELL. No frills. No welcoming words like, *Come on in and look around.* No one walked along the sidewalk. I suspected there was life inside the shop due to the OPEN sign and a light I could see through the dirty windows. I understood why Harvey's mother was worried. The place showed every sign of a struggling business.

I was about to get out of my vehicle and go inside when the door to the shop opened and Rick Stapleton walked out. More like stormed out. His face was flushed and his hands were fists. He strode by me, not glancing into my Jeep. Rick's intense stare was only for the sidewalk ahead and whatever or whoever he was seeing in his mind. His lips were set in a grim straight line.

What was the one-time employee of Alexander Koskov doing at the competitor's place of business? I hoped I'd find out.

I watched him in my rearview mirror. When I saw him turn the corner and disappear from sight, I got out and headed for the store. A sign supporting a school fund-raiser had been taped to the glass-front door.

I entered and saw a plump man talking to an elderly woman, who stood next to a chair. I wandered around the aisles filled with odds and ends of furniture. They weren't the high quality I'd seen at Alexander's. Definitely no museum pieces were in evidence. I'd call what I was seeing secondhand furniture, not antiques. Numerous pieces had scratches and no one had dusted in a while. A hint of mustiness hung in the air.

Alexander hadn't been in the area long. The shabbiness I saw here had taken time to accumulate. I'd say the business had been off-track for a while. I doubted getting his coin customers back would help much. On the other hand, losing them could have meant the business going belly up.

A counter ran the length of the store, over half of it glass-covered. I went to check it out and found a gun display in the first section. A heavy wire grid had been installed under the glass. Any thoughts of a smash and grab were out of the question.

I was familiar with handguns, more so with rifles. Back on the family ranch, we carried handguns with us when we were out in the back pastures in case of an animal attack. We used rifles first, if possible, but there wasn't always time to get them out of the scabbard. Luckily, shooting the gun in the air had been sufficient for me to scare them off so far.

There were some interesting pieces. A small derringer with an ivory handle caught my eye. Pretty, but it would be of no help dealing with a charging wolf if it came to that. The guns appeared to range from modern to ones that had been around for a while.

The next section of the counter had coins on display. Harvey hadn't taken the precaution that Alexander had by showing only photos. Maybe he didn't feel he had to because of his counter setup. Gold and silver coins from numerous countries formed rows on faded green velvet. The dates ranged from recent to over a hundred years old.

I wandered closer to the man and woman as I browsed. The woman wore a long brown skirt and a loose-fitting black blouse. Deep wrinkles crisscrossed her cheeks. A black-fringed satin shawl covered her dowager's hump. Its pattern of red, pink, and yellow roses added a splash of color and a cheerful note to an otherwise drab scene.

The man's once-white shirt, now dingy, stretched tightly over his middle. A few brown drops on the front of it were probably coffee from the stained mug he held. His dark brown hair was brushed back from his forehead, emphasizing his bushy eyebrows.

The man turned to me. "I'll be with you in a few minutes, miss. I'm Harvey Goldstein, the owner of the store. If you're interested in coins, I can show you more than what's out here."

"Thanks," I replied.

He turned back to the woman. "Gladys, this is the same conversation we had yesterday. I told you thirty dollars. That's it."

"Well, I thought maybe you needed the money more today and you'd be willing to let me have it for twenty-five," she replied.

"I won't sell at a loss." He clamped his lips closed.

She had a fierce scowl for a wizened little old lady. Harvey should maybe think twice. I glanced at the chair—a rattan rocker. I could see one corner on the back where the material was beginning to come apart. It looked comfortable, and I could imagine Gladys in it.

"Can you hold it for me until my check comes at the end of the month?" she asked in a high-pitched voice.

His face softened. "I'll tell you what. If someone wants to buy it before then, I'll call you for first dibs. However, if they offer me more than the thirty dollars I've been asking for it, that's what I'll expect you to pay."

Gladys nodded. "Fair enough."

"You could borrow the money from your son. Ronnie's restaurant's been doing well."

She squared her shoulders and her chin jutted out. "I don't ask for any favors from him. I take care of myself." Gladys picked up her purse, which had been resting on the counter. "I'll see you at the end of the month."

With that, she turned and headed out the door.

Harvey sighed and joined me at the counter. "How can I help you?"

I dug in my purse and pulled out the pouch Rudy had given me. "I recently inherited a few coins. Here's one of them."

I put the silver disc on the counter. Harvey picked it up and examined it. Beads of sweat popped out on his brow. He pulled a handkerchief out of his pocket, dabbed his face, and shoved it back into his jeans.

"I can give you eighteen hundred dollars for it."

I feigned surprise. "Is that all? Alexander Koskov offered me twenty-one hundred."

Harvey's features hardened. "Well, he's dead, so he isn't going to give that amount for it now."

I continued with my act. "Dead? What happened?"

His eyes narrowed. "It's all over town. I'm surprised you don't know."

"I'm new to the area. The newspaper only comes out once a week, on Tuesday. I saw Alexander on Wednesday, so it wouldn't have been in the paper yet."

He nodded. "You're right." He put my coin on the counter. "He was murdered. Found at the marina. Shot. No one has been arrested yet."

"Oh my gosh. That's awful. It's strange to think of him as dead when I only saw him a short time ago."

Now what? I decided to take a different tactic with my charade.

"I'm big-time into crime shows but have never been close to a real murder before. Wasn't that one of his employees who left your store just now? I thought I recognized him from when I met with Alexander."

Okay. That wasn't the truth, but this was all an act anyway.

"Yeah. Rick Stapleton. Tried to sell me a gold coin. I recognized it as a type I buy from a couple of Russian guys. Said Koskov gave it to him. Fat chance of that. More likely he stole it. It's a very expensive coin."

"Wow! Do you think Alexander caught him, and maybe the guy killed him?"

"Don't know. Don't care. Just know I don't want that coin anywhere near me. The police questioned me, and I don't want to give them any reason to think I had anything to do with the murder. That coin would be on Koskov's inventory list, along with a photograph."

"Gee, what are you going to do? Are you going to tell the police?" *Ugh. I didn't know how long I could keep up this gushing mystery fan act.*

Harvey's smile was a self-satisfied smirk. I sensed he liked being the center of my attention.

"You bet. And I told Rick that, too. He didn't like it one bit. Too bad. Here he's a local, lived in the area for years. He pointed people in Alexander's direction, a newcomer, rather than helping me. I've been here all my life."

Harvey's face reddened as he talked. He shook his head. "Even dead, the guy is messing with me."

"What do you mean?"

"Alexander stole my customers, and now I'm getting pulled into his murder investigation." He pushed Rudy's coin in my direction. "Do you want to sell this to me?"

"Let me think about it. I just received them and started checking into their value."

"The price fluctuates daily. Deciding when to sell is a bit like gambling. Will you get more the next day or less? Don't let what Koskov offered you influence your decision. I don't know how he could pay some of the prices he did."

"Thanks. You've been really helpful." I tucked the coin back in the pouch and into my purse. "You're doing the right thing. Calling the police and all."

It was a relief to exit the dreary store. I hurried to my Jeep. With Harvey's business in such poor shape, losing valuable customers gave him a stronger motive for killing Alexander. Had he decided he wasn't going to lose any more buyers? But why kill him on Rudy and Ivan's boat?

I started the engine and turned up the heater a notch. I needed some extra warmth after that encounter. I headed out of town, then saw the sign for the marina. On impulse, I decided to stop to see if Joe had any news that might be helpful, considering he was now the unofficial crime reporter for the area.

I found an end spot in the lot and pulled in. I glanced at the white van on my right and noticed numerous door dings. One rusty dent had the word *ouch* written next to it in black ink. I repositioned my Jeep so I was farther away from the vehicle. Whoever drove it clearly didn't care about doors banging into the side of it.

I headed for the bait shop. A gentle breeze carried a slight smell of fish but, luckily, not as strong as the other day.

I spotted Joe in his usual attire and place—bib overalls and rocking chair. "Hey, Joe."

"Hey back to you." He leaned over and peered around me toward the parking lot.

I looked over my shoulder but didn't see anything in the lot. "Are you looking for something or expecting someone?"

"Just checkin' to see if the cop cars arrived yet. They have every time you've showed up." He chuckled, a dry, cackling sound.

"I hate to disappoint you, but no police today."

Then I heard the sirens.

Joe sat back with a satisfied smile.

I turned to look at the entrance to the marina. Two police cars approached, lights flashing and sirens blaring.

Now what?

Chapter 18

The cop cars passed through the parking lot, stopping at the far end of the marina. There were some large buildings located there, used by commercial fishermen according to the signs I'd seen as I'd driven in.

My turn to smile. "Not me this time, Joe."

"Girl, you're a magnet. I'll find out what that's about later. Thanks for bringin' them while I'm out here to watch."

"I did *not* bring them!"

"Sure you did." He gave me a wink. "You're connected, just don't know it."

I wasn't going to pursue this any further. "I was in the area and decided to see if you had learned anything else." I looked at him. "From what I understand, you've dubbed yourself the local unofficial crime reporter."

He chuckled again. "Hey, you've been givin' me more entertainment than any TV show. Others deserve to know about what's goin' on."

"A murder isn't what I'd call entertainment," I said.

His smile faded. "You're right there. The dagger was interestin'. Glad to hear it wasn't real blood."

I wasn't going to ask how he knew. The town communication just operated that way.

"Did you know Koskov?"

Joe rubbed his chin. "Had some encounters with him but wouldn't wish him dead."

"Do you mind telling me what kind of incidents?"

"Nah. I know you're helpin' the brothers out. Alexander was a cheap son of a gun. I arrange fishin' trips, and he wanted to put together one for some friends. Tried to knock me down in price...got angry when I wouldn't budge."

"I heard he had a temper."

"Another time, he wanted money back for some bait he bought. Said it wasn't any good. I told him the bait was fine and it was the person doin' the fishin' that wasn't any good."

I raised my eyebrows. "I'm going to guess that got him angry."

"Oh, yeah. Couple of my buddies came out of the store when he started rantin.'" Joe laughed. "Two Paul Bunyan types. One of them held up the string of fish he'd caught usin' the same bait Koskov was tryin' to return. That put a stop to Alexander."

"Thanks, Joe." I gave him my business card. "You're right. I am trying to help Rudy and Ivan. If you hear anything that might be helpful, please call me."

"Will do. And I'll let you know what your cop buddies are here for."

I shook my head. He wasn't going to let it go. I waved good-bye, walked to my vehicle, and returned to the inn. The clock in the kitchen showed me I had about half an hour to grab a bite to eat before joining the Sentinels. I fixed a sandwich, checked my emails, and headed for the meeting room. Once there, I pulled out our charts and hung them on the walls.

As usual, Helen had put out coffee, tea, and water. This time she'd added some baklava. I knew the Silver Sentinels would appreciate that. Everyone arrived over the course of the next ten minutes. Mary had no dog purse today.

"Is Princess still visiting with Sargent?" I asked.

Mary nodded. "The dogs enjoy playing together...except for when Sargent gets too close to Princess's green stuffed frog, her favorite toy."

Princess wore jeweled collars and frilly coats, but she was a force to be reckoned with. I was sure Sargent wasn't about to take her frog.

Mary headed for the baklava. "I didn't bring any sweets today. Helen called to tell me she'd put out some of the Russian delicacy she's been baking." She put a piece on a plate and took a sniff. "I love the sweet smell of the honey. I'm really looking forward to trying some."

"I had a taste, and the pastry is delicious," I said.

After the group got their food and drink, everyone sat, and Gertie picked up her gavel. She brought it down with a loud bang. "Let's start the meeting. So, what have we learned? Who wants to go first?"

I volunteered and shared what I'd found out and observed—as well as suspected--on my visits to Tom and Harvey. Rudy continued in his role as recorder.

"They both have strong motives and exhibit a lot of anger," I said.

Gertie nodded. "Confirms what we suspected."

I went to pour myself some coffee. "I also decided to stop by to see Joe at the bait shop."

The Professor picked up his pen and twirled it idly through his fingers. "What did our crime reporter have to say?"

"Besides hinting I have powers to attract the police, not anything that moves our search for the murderer forward. He confirmed that Koskov had a temper and shared a couple of his run-ins with me. I gave him my card and asked him to call if he learned anything."

Ivan put down his piece of baklava. "Man with temper could have many enemies."

"I agree with Ivan," the Professor said. "The more we learn about Koskov, the more suspects we might find."

"Rudy, did you ever have any negative interactions with Alexander?" I asked.

Rudy shook his head. "No. He was always a polite businessman. Besides, there was nothing for us to argue about. He offered me a price, and it was always a good one. I got the money and he got the coin he wanted."

Gertie turned to Mary. "What did you find out about Alena?"

I knew there was a surprise in store for the Sentinels. Mary enjoyed being an actress at times and didn't miss this opportunity to bring a little drama to the scene. She peered at each Sentinel individually, then said two words.

"Russian Mafia."

The room exploded with comments and questions, everyone talking at once.

Gertie rapped the gavel a couple of times and people quieted down. "Let's save the questions until Mary has told us what she knows."

"Her father is Boris Baranov," Mary continued, "and he's in prison for crimes he committed in connection with the Russian Mafia. Alena lives in a gated community in San Francisco called Applegate, which I believe is owned by her father. Her office is there as well. There is a very high level of security."

"How did you find out about the place?" I asked.

"I located Alena's address, then checked the Internet to find out more about the area. I got the name of the community and looked at the application form and its board members. Her father is president."

"Do you think it's an area where Mafia families live?" the Professor asked.

"No, I think it's just the opposite. People are screened in order to live there. The rules state that anyone with a criminal record will not be accepted."

Gertie tilted her head. "Sounds like he's trying to create a safe environment for his daughter."

Mary nodded. "Alena's mother was killed in a hit-and-run accident when Alena was a child. The police never found out who did it or if it was intentional. It might have been in retaliation for something Boris did. Shortly after it happened, Alena was sent to boarding school in Switzerland and began using a different last name."

"Do you feel she's close to her father?" I asked.

"I do," Mary said. "He visited her in Europe frequently, and they always spent her vacations together."

"Do you think she works with the Mafia?" Gertie asked.

"I didn't find anything that would make me think that. It seems like Alena's father kept her as far away from what he was doing as possible. I called her office and spoke with a friendly woman who is going to mail me information about the services Alena offers."

"Good work, Mary," Gertie said. "You've learned a lot."

"I did a quick check on Alena last night," I said. "I knew about the father. Even though he's in prison, he might have some connection with what has happened. I think we should put him on the chart."

Everyone nodded, and Boris became a suspect.

"My turn," Gertie said. "I spoke with Harvey's mother again. She was embarrassed that maybe her comments had made her sound happy someone had murdered Alexander."

"Which they did," Mary mumbled as she stood and went for another piece of baklava.

"I agree, Mary," Gertie said.

The Professor stopped playing with his pen and put it down. "Is she a possible suspect?"

Gertie shook her head. "Highly unlikely. If Alexander was killed someplace else, she wouldn't have the strength to move his body. I also don't know how she could lure him to the *Nadia*. She's never mentioned anything about boats, so I doubt if she has any familiarity with the marina."

The Professor looked at the brothers. "Do either of you know her?"

They both shook their heads.

"I think we should put her name down at the bottom. We won't focus on her, but let's keep her in the picture," the Professor said.

"Her name is Frances Goldstein," Gertie said, and Rudy added her to our suspect list.

"Did you have any luck, Professor?" I asked.

He sighed. "Very little. There are layers of ownership associated with the company on the lease, the Williams Corporation. That in and of itself isn't necessarily suspicious with the way companies are being bought up by giant conglomerations. However, it's possible there has been some intentional covering up."

"What about Vladimir?" I asked.

"I looked into him. Vladimir handles real estate, but I couldn't track him to that company. I'll keep digging. I also thought I'd call to see if they'd be interested in talking to me about buying them out of their lease. They have four months paid in advance."

"That makes sense," Gertie said. "You might be able to glean something from the person-to-person interaction."

The Professor nodded. "That's what I was thinking."

Mary shifted in her chair. "I suspect Alena's father is in to real estate because of the community she lives in. You might want to pursue him as being behind the lease."

The Professor made a note. "I'll do that."

Mary placed a third piece of baklava on her plate. "This is so good. I'll have to get Helen's recipe." She turned to the Professor. "I'll do more checking on Alena. Under her list of services as a financial planner, real estate investment is listed. I'll see if there are any ties to the company you've been researching."

"We have something to add," Rudy said. "The police let us know we could go back on the *Nadia*. We did that this morning and found Rick Stapleton camping out on our boat."

"Yah. I throw him off," Ivan said.

"Daniel said he often makes himself a houseguest," I said. "Sounds like your vacant boat met his needs."

Rudy added the information about Rick.

Gertie looked at our lists and frowned. "Not a lot of next steps, but we need to keep pushing ahead with what we've got."

"Gertie," Mary said, "why don't you and I take a trip to Harvey Goldstein's shop? We can go antique hunting. It's not much of a plan, but you never know when something might come our way."

"Okay," Gertie said. "I'll call you later, and we can set a time."

Rudy updated the Next Steps list.

"Tomorrow is the Russian festival," I said. "Let's keep our eyes and ears open. A number of people who knew Alexander will be there. Talk of his murder is likely to happen."

"What about next meeting?" Ivan asked.

"Let's plan on Sunday," I said, "unless we find out something important and decide to call an emergency meeting tomorrow."

"It'll have to be in the afternoon," Rudy said. "We're having tea with Timur and Verushka."

"Will four o'clock Sunday work?" Gertie asked.

Everyone nodded and the gavel dropped.

I gave back Rudy his coin and went to change for the tracking training with Gus. Whoever employed Alexander didn't trust him, considering the hidden cameras. That person or group could be a key piece to the puzzle. Had they caught Alexander stealing from them? And what about the boxes he was so secretive about? Was he bringing in something illegally? If so, he would've been recorded in action. Had he been killed because of what was on the cameras? Was someone from the Williams Corporation responsible for his murder?

If Rick had stolen the coin he'd tried to sell to Harvey, that would show up as well. Was he in danger? We needed to find out who was behind the lease as soon as possible.

Chapter 19

I changed into jeans, then put on high-topped hiking boots. I didn't know if we'd be walking through tick country. The more I thought about Rick, the more concerned I became that he was in danger and needed to be warned. I texted Daniel to ask if he could come over at three thirty instead of the three forty-five we had agreed upon for dropping off Allie. He immediately replied that that would work.

My cell phone rang. I didn't recognize the number. "Hello."

"Hey there, Kelly. Joe here."

"Hi, Joe. What's up?"

"I'm a man of my word. Found out what the police were here for."

"Why were they there?"

"Nothin' to do with the goings on you've been involved in. Been a lot of vehicle break-ins lately. Cops tracked a couple of guys to a room they rented in the warehouse. Found a stash of loot."

"Thanks for letting me know. Anything new that might help the brothers?" I asked.

"Nah. But I'll let you know if I hear anythin'."

"Thanks."

We ended the call. I glanced at my watch and saw I'd be right on time for my meeting with Alena. I wanted to question her about Alexander and the leasing company but, as always, there was the question of how to begin. I hoped an answer would present itself.

In the kitchen, I filled a metal travel mug with water and put it in the refrigerator. I'd take it with me to the tracking session. At the sound of a car in the driveway, I glanced out the side window and saw Alena drive in.

I know my horse breeds, but cars not so much. I knew this was no equivalent to a draft horse designed to pull a wagon of supplies or a load of kids. The sporty two-seater was more of a sleek Arabian, delicate-looking but fast and strong. The sun glinted off its pearlescent exterior.

Alena emerged and headed toward the guest path, her long black skirt swirling around black leather boots. A red sweater over a black top stopped just at her hips and was held together by a single silver button. I lost sight of her as she went around the corner, and I headed for the front door to greet her.

The doorbell rang. When I got there, I saw Alena through the window, alongside the door. She had her back to me, gazing out at the nearby Pacific Ocean. A breeze ruffled her blond hair.

I opened the door. "Hi, Alena."

She turned toward me. "I never get tired of looking at the sea…the constant movement, the changing colors, the different emotions the water can convey."

Alena entered, and her perfume mingling with the fragrance of the flowers framing the porch brought a cloud of sweet scent wafting in after her.

"I know what you mean." I closed the door behind her. "Calm and placid swells to angry waves dashing against the cliffs."

"Well said, Kelly. You could be a writer."

"Not me. Too much computer time. I grew up on a ranch where action was the ruling word of each and every day." I smiled. "Thanks for the compliment, though. Would you like something to drink?"

"No, thanks. I just finished lunch with Vladimir. We had some final loose ends to tie up."

"Let's go to the conference room."

We walked down the hallway, and Alena stopped at the entrance and read the plaque over the door. "The Silver Sentinels. Who are they?"

"A crime-solving group of senior citizens. Come on in, and I'll tell you about them." *My chance. An explanation and a segue to the current case.*

"They're five wonderful people who work to keep their community safe and help their friends. I'm an honorary member." I pointed to my red hair. "My hair isn't the right shade as yet."

We sat down across from each other at the conference table.

Alena laughed. "Silver hair is one of the prerequisites?"

I nodded. "Yes. That's the reason for their name. They're working on a couple of cases right now—one of them being Alexander's murder."

Alena frowned. "That sounds more like a job for the police, not a group of seniors."

"I believe you know Rudy and Ivan Doblinsky, who are on the Russian Heritage Committee."

"Yes. I've talked to them briefly."

"They're both Silver Sentinels. Alexander's body was found on their boat."

Alena nodded. "Helping their own. I understand now. How do they work?"

I explained how we gathered information and took roles appropriate to where we could be the most useful. The length of time the Sentinels had been in the community gave them advantages that not even the police had in terms of connections.

"One of them is researching Alexander, as well as the leasing company he worked for, which is based in San Francisco. We're looking in to possible leads there." *And another is gathering information about you.*

She straightened a bit. She stared at me for a few moments, as if trying to make up her mind, toying with a pendant attached to the gold omega encircling her neck. Its solitaire diamond glinted in the light. "If you're doing research about people who knew Alexander and are part of the San Francisco scene, you probably know by now my father is in jail for supposedly being part of the Russian Mafia."

I stiffened, and my breathing became rapid and shallow. We'd been investigating the daughter of a possible Mafia boss. My face grew warm.

I nodded. "We only checked on you because of Alexander and San Francisco. Not because we suspect you of anything."

"I understand. I would do the same thing, especially for friends. You must be thorough."

I relaxed, and my shoulders, which had inched up, dropped back into place. "I'm glad you feel that way. Asking questions and digging into people's backgrounds is very uncomfortable for me, but I'll do what I need to do to help those I care about."

"People who have you for a friend are very fortunate." She examined her crimson nails. "What would you like to know?"

"Do you know anything about Alexander that might help us to understand why he was murdered or who killed him?"

"No. I had very little interaction with him. My first encounter with Alexander happened when my father and I were dining in a restaurant and Alexander came up and spoke to my father about meeting him the next day. After he left, my father apologized for the interruption and said he would speak to Alexander about it. My father keeps his business as far away from me as possible."

Alexander had a connection with Boris!

"Did Alexander ever mention anything to you about what he did for your father?"

"No. The next time I saw Alexander was at the first committee meeting I attended. He never mentioned my father's name or referred to the incident at the restaurant. We both treated it as if it never happened."

"Do you know if your father had any connection with Alexander's business here?"

Touchy ground here…but it could be a legitimate connection.

She shook her head. "He's busy working on getting the alleged charges against him dropped and getting out of jail." Alena paused. "We're in regular communication. I can ask him if he knows anything."

"I'd appreciate that. Every scrap of information we can gather is important to us." Now it was my turn to pause. "It sounds like you two are close. It must be hard for you, having him locked up."

"My mother was killed when I was a child. My father sent me to a boarding school in Switzerland. He bought a home near it, and we spent as much time together there as possible…vacations and an occasional weekend. He still had his business in San Francisco to attend to."

"I'm sorry about the loss of your mother."

She nodded. "Father tried hard to take her place, fill her shoes as you Americans say. We cooked together, and he taught me many of the traditional Russian recipes."

"Thoughtful of him," I said. "Do you have any brothers or sisters?"

"No. I am an only child."

Time to steer away from her personal life. "Do you know of any friends or acquaintances Alexander had on the committee?"

"He didn't associate with people much during the meetings. Vladimir is the only one I can think of who he spent any time with. Have you talked to him?"

"I have. He says he didn't really know Alexander that well."

Alena leaned back. "Let's talk of other things. A meeting to schedule and a Russian formal ball to organize."

I stood and went to the chart on the wall. "We have the room calendar on our computers, but I like to keep a physical one in here. It makes it easy for a quick check, and to know what's needed when."

We looked at a couple of dates and decided on next Saturday.

"I'd like to book a room for myself here as well for Friday and Saturday night," Alena said.

I'd recently checked the guest schedule and knew we had space. "I can do that for you."

Alena pulled out her checkbook. "The same amount as last time for the conference room?"

"Yes." I penciled in Russian Heritage Committee.

She filled out the check and handed it to me. "We will debrief the festival and begin plans for the ball." Her eyes sparkled. "It should be wonderful. It'll be like a royal ball of old. Long gowns and satin gloves. Men in tuxedos."

Long formal gowns. Yep. I have a number of those in my closet, as well as a drawer full of satin gloves. Yep. Right up my alley. In truth, the only gloves I have with me are my leather ones for riding.

"You will come, right? It'll be held at the community center. That handsome man who runs it will be there." She gave me a coy look. "The contract had the same company name as your inn, Resorts International. Surely you must know him."

"Scott Thompson. He's a friend of mine." I felt another blush on the way.

Alena tilted her head. "A friend of the type you wouldn't mind having me get to know, or a friend you'd like to keep to yourself?"

My face felt hot. "Scott and I aren't a couple, if that's what you mean."

I had started to say *not dating*, but I think we'd crossed that line a bit.

"Good," Alena said. "I look forward to getting to know him better."

I didn't know what kind of emotion shot through my body, but it wasn't a happy one.

I looked at the clock on the wall and stood. "I have another meeting. I'm glad we were able to find a date that works for you. Thank you for all the information you shared and offering to talk with your father."

She stood as well and picked up her red leather purse with a designer logo on the side. "I'm happy to help. A murderer on the loose does not help our festival any. I hope you find the person responsible."

I accompanied her to the front door, then went to the work area. Allie and Daniel were there, along with Helen. Tommy entered a few minutes later with Fred attired in what I knew to be a tracking harness.

"Why the equipment on Fred?" I asked Tommy.

"I want him to know today is about business. He needs to watch and pay attention."

That actually made more sense than maybe he realized. I'd read that service dogs knew when their harness or vest was put on, it was time to work.

"You have about fifteen minutes before you have to leave," Daniel said. "Why don't you go outside and practice with Fred a little bit?"

"Okay. Come on, Allie. You helped me before. You can hide, and I'll tell Fred to find you."

Tommy raced to the door, along with Fred. Allie followed at a more leisurely pace.

Helen pulled crackers down from the cupboard and began preparing the evening trays. "Thanks for taking Tommy to the training. I'll get the afternoon guest appetizers ready."

"Works for me," I said. "Do you want any coffee, Daniel?"

"No, thanks." Daniel gestured with his head toward the worktable. "Let's sit down. I have a few things to share with you, and I know you wanted to talk about Rick."

"Sure. Let me grab my water." I pulled the cold container out of the refrigerator and joined him.

Daniel sat at the end of the table. "Stanton came by and used my phone to call Rick Stapleton. Rick answered and Stanton set up a time to see him. Stapleton called and was none too happy about the situation. Asked me if I told the police about Alexander's accusations about him stealing. I told him no."

"I can fill you in on how the police found out. Deputy Stanton came by after one of the Silver Sentinel meetings and before I took the charts down. He saw what we'd written under Rick's name. Said the possible theft was new information for him."

"I figured it was something like that but didn't tell Rick anything." Daniel leaned forward and put his arms on the table. "I asked him where he was living now, but his answer was evasive. Something about here and there."

I sipped my water. "He's been on Rudy and Ivan's boat."

"What?"

I filled him in on what had happened at the marina, then told him what I'd observed and heard at Harvey's shop. "It sounds like Alexander's suspicions might have been correct. Did you notice on our charts about the two sets of surveillance cameras in the shop?"

"No. I really didn't look at them. Wanted to give you my news and go get Allie."

"There was one obvious set of cameras and one that appeared to be for watching the employees without their knowledge. Turns out, the shop wasn't Alexander's," I said. "He'd been hired to run it. If he was stealing, his employer probably knows...and would know if Rick stole anything as well, if in fact he did."

"Do you think whoever is behind the cameras killed Alexander?"
"Possibly."
"Then that would put Rick in danger as well," Daniel stated.
I nodded. "That's what I was thinking."
A shiver of apprehension ran through me.

Chapter 20

"Will you call Rick to warn him?" I asked.

Daniel pulled out his phone, looking troubled. "There's no way Rick would answer his phone now once he sees my number. Not after what happened with Stanton."

I handed him my cell phone. "Use mine."

Daniel took it, looked Rick up in his contact list, then punched in numbers on my phone. After a couple of moments, Daniel shook his head. I figured he was going to have to leave a message.

"Rick, I know you're mad at me. I thought you wouldn't answer if you saw my number, so I'm using Kelly's phone in the hope that I'd be able to talk to you. She and the Silver Sentinels are investigating Koskov's murder."

The Sentinels had been in the paper enough times, most locals would know who they were.

"There's a possibility you might be in danger. You can call either one of us back to learn more. Just so you know, Kelly has more details than I do. Be careful and watch your back." He handed my phone back to me.

I was relieved Daniel had made the call. I didn't like Rick after everything I'd seen and heard, plus trespassing on the boat. However, I didn't wish him dead. My goal was to prevent another murder.

"Let's both keep an eye out for him," I said. "Even if he stole the coin, it doesn't mean he should pay for it with his life, if that's a possibility."

"I agree," Daniel stood. "And thanks for giving Allie a ride to watch Gus train. She's been really excited about going."

"Sure. I'm happy to take her. Stanton said the practice would last about an hour. We should be back here by five fifteen."

"See you then," Daniel said.

"Okay."

"Bye, Helen," he said and left.

I grabbed my jacket off the hook by the back door and put it over my arm. "Helen, I'll see you in a little over an hour."

She looked over her shoulder from where she stood at the sink and nodded. "Thanks again for helping with Tommy."

Tommy and Fred were in the parking lot. From my vantage point on the back porch, I saw Allie crouched on the other side of the inn's red Toyota pickup, out of sight of the basset hound and his owner.

Tommy held Allie's jacket out to Fred. The dog took a sniff and looked at him.

"Track Allie, Fred. Track her," Tommy commanded.

Fred looked around, then raised his nose. I could see his nostrils working overtime. He didn't put his nose to the ground. Instead, he trotted to the truck and around the side.

"You found me, Fred." Allie gave him a hug.

There was a little water on the top of my travel glass. I rolled my finger in it and held it up to check the direction of the wind. Just what I figured. Fred hadn't tracked the path Allie took; he could smell her from the wind going under the truck and straight to that active nose of his. I wouldn't tell the kids. No reason to disappoint them.

We all piled into my Jeep and headed for the training area located in a nearby state park. As I approached, I saw Stanton standing next to a police vehicle parked in the lot. We drove in, and I pulled up next to him. Tommy jumped out with Fred in tow. Stanton opened the back door of his car. Gus slid to the ground and went to welcome Fred.

Allie and I joined them.

"Tommy, you mentioned you trained Fred for tracking," Deputy Stanton said.

The ten-year-old nodded vigorously. "Just a little. We're real beginners."

Stanton smiled at him. "How did you learn how to train him?"

"I researched online and read a lot. Mom bought me a special harness for my birthday, and I taught Allie how to put down the trail for me."

"I brought some hot-dog pieces," Stanton said. "Why don't you show me what you, Allie, and Fred do?"

Both kids nodded energetically. Allie took off one of her shoes, pulled off her sock, and handed it to Tommy. Then she slipped her bare foot back into her tennis shoe. Stanton pulled a small ice chest from the back of the car.

He took out a container and held it out to Allie. "Here are nickel-size pieces of hot dog. Take as many as you want. The bait has already been put out for Gus." Stanton pointed to an area a short distance away. "There's a flat, grassy area over there. That'll be a good spot for the three of you to work."

Allie took a handful of coin-size pieces of meat. All of us walked over to the place Stanton had indicated.

Allie put several pieces of hot dog a couple of feet in front of Fred, where he could see them. Then she walked out a couple of feet, carefully placing one foot in front of the other, creating a single track. She mashed the grass a little by moving her foot from side to side.

Tommy said to Stanton, "I learned the dogs use both the crushed grass and the person's scent for tracking."

Stanton nodded. "That's right, Tommy."

Allie put down several more pieces of meat. She repeated this process three times. At the last stop she created a small pile of hot-dog coins. Allie then turned to the left and walked at a right angle for about six feet and then turned and walked back toward us, staying at a distance from the track she had put down.

"Impressive," Stanton said. "You learned all of this on the computer and from reading books, Tommy?"

"Yeah, mostly. I love learning. I really got in to it. I also emailed a woman who trains dogs used by the police in Oregon." He stopped for a minute, a worried look on his face. "Deputy Stanton, I know you've told me not to email strangers. Mom checked her out and said it was okay."

Stanton smiled. "I'm glad you remembered that."

"Mom got all the books that had anything to do with dog tracking out of the library."

Stanton laughed. "You were thorough!"

Fred tugged at his leash. The hot dogs were calling to him.

Tommy held Allie's sock out to him to sniff. "Track."

The basset hound gobbled the first batch of treats, then put his nose to the ground, casting his head from side to side. He slowly followed Allie's footsteps, Tommy behind him with a loose leash. The kids clapped and cheered each time he located the bait. When he got to the last one, they really whooped it up.

Tommy and Fred came running back to Allie and Stanton. "Everything I read said to make a big deal of it when he finds the last pile."

"That's right. It's part of the reward," Deputy Stanton said. "You two are doing a great job."

Tommy handed Allie her sock. "I know the next step is to keep widening the distance, and there are things you can do to make it even harder."

Stanton nodded and pointed up the hill. "Now, let's see how Gus does."

I noticed there were pieces of wire with yellow flags on them at various spots.

He continued. "Those flags mark the path Gus needs to take to get to the final reward. There are some obstacles in his way, and the path is a winding one. Because he's not used to working with me, I made it easier and used more rewards than would happen with his owner. I want it to be a successful experience for him."

He pulled a small notebook and a pen out of his pocket.

"What's that for?" Tommy asked.

"We keep a detailed diary of all training sessions. It helps us know what to work on next and has even been useful in some trials to validate the dog's tracking ability."

Stanton bent down and held out a T-shirt to the dog. Gus rooted his nose in the fabric, then looked at Stanton.

"I hired a high school student to put down the track and this is his shirt." Stanton looked at the dog. "Track, Gus."

Tommy sat next to Fred and gave his own command. "Watch Gus, Fred."

Over the course of the next forty-five minutes, we watched as Gus sniffed and slowly walked upward. Stanton kept his distance with a long leash, sticking to the dog's pace. Occasionally, he made a note in the journal.

Tracking wasn't the all-out run you often saw portrayed on television. When Gus reached the final flag, we yelled out words of praise. Fred jumped up and down with his front end.

Stanton came down the hill, part walking, part sliding on the steep hill and slick grass.

"That was fun," Tommy said. "Seeing it is a lot better than just reading about it."

"Gus's owner has been working on a new command with him. He tells Gus *hold*, and that's his cue to stand on someone. Tommy, would you be willing to be the victim, so to speak?"

Tommy handed Fred's leash to Allie and sprawled on the ground before Stanton could finish his sentence.

"Gus," Stanton said to the dog.

The bloodhound looked at him, all attention.

Stanton pointed to Tommy. "Hold."

The dog obligingly stepped onto Tommy with all four feet. The hound bent down his head, and his long ears tickled Tommy's face. The boy began giggling. Gus gave him a big, slurpy kiss. Tommy laughed harder, and we all joined in.

"Gus, off," Stanton commanded.

The dog obeyed but now was in to giving Tommy large, sloppy kisses. Tommy's face started to turn red from laughing so hard.

"Gus, heel," Stanton said.

The dog did as commanded.

Tommy sat up, and when he seemed to have regained his breath, Stanton said, "How about you kids go collect the flags?"

"Sure," Allie said.

They both raced off, Fred in tow, the steep hill meaning very little with their youthful energy.

"Gus, down."

The dog obliged by going into a traditional down position, resting on his haunches. Then he gave a groan, rolled over on his side, and stretched out. It appeared to be rest time.

Stanton turned to me. "Thanks for letting me know about Daniel and Rick's conversation. I was able to reach Rick using Daniel's phone. I had him come to the station and questioned him today."

"Daniel told me. Rick called him and let him know he wasn't happy about the ruse."

"Too bad. Rick could've handled it a different way. Claims he didn't get the messages." Stanton shook his head. "Like I'm going to believe that." He paused. "Do you have anything new to share?"

I told him about my experience at the coin shop.

Stanton's face darkened. "Rick didn't say anything about a coin. Denied he'd taken anything. I guess technically he didn't have to mention it, if he's sticking to the story it was given to him. It'll be interesting to see his reaction when I ask him why Alexander gave the man he fired an expensive gift."

"Rudy and Ivan encountered him on their boat. It seems he's been living there."

Stanton took out the notepad he used during investigations and wrote in it. "The word *trespass* might help to get him to talk."

Tommy and Allie returned, out of breath but laughing, each clasping a bunch of wired flags. Fred plopped down on the ground, panting harder than either of them.

"Why don't you kids take those over to the patrol car? You can put them on the ground next to it," Stanton said. "Allie, do you want to take Gus? He and Fred can have a little playtime while I finish talking with Ms. Jackson."

Allie's face brightened. "You bet."

She grabbed the long lead that Stanton had coiled up. I wasn't sure how much play was left in Fred as he plodded behind the kids.

"Anything else I should know about?" Stanton asked.

"Probably nothing you don't already know."

I shared with him about the Mafia connection, Tom's bitterness, and Harvey's struggles. I was right—no new news for him.

"For not being connected to the police, you all are amazing at what you can dig up."

"We're really stuck on finding out who owns the Williams Company." I looked at him hopefully.

Stanton put away his notes. "Sorry. I know you've helped me out a lot on this one, but I can't talk about it."

"I understand. Just thought I'd give it a try."

"With as much as you've accomplished already, I'm guessing you'll find out," he said.

That gave me some hope that learning who was behind the company was discoverable if we just kept at it.

Stanton's phone rang. He listened for a few minutes. "Got it. On my way."

He put his phone away. "You'll know this soon enough with the speed with which news gets around Redwood Cove." He paused. "Looks like I won't be asking Rick Stapleton about the coin."

I looked at him questioningly.

"He's been murdered. His body was found on the *Nadia*."

Chapter 21

A jolt of shock raced through me. "What?" It was almost a shout.

Stanton's face had a grim set to it. "Shot. One of the boat owners saw the body on the deck and called it in."

Despair followed my initial reaction. "I was too late."

Stanton frowned. "What do you mean?"

"I started to wonder if Alexander had been murdered because he might have been stealing from the Williams Company, which meant Rick might be in danger as well. I had Daniel call to warn him."

"Don't go racing to conclusions and blaming yourself. You don't know if this has anything to do with what happened to Alexander."

I sighed. "You're right. It's just that Daniel called him a little over an hour ago, so it's fresh on my mind."

"I don't have the exact time of death yet, but from what I was told, I'm guessing he was dead when the message was left. Even if we find out his death is connected to Alexander and the Williams Company, you can't blame yourself for not figuring out something sooner. Life doesn't work that way." He snorted. "I'd go crazy if I blamed myself for everything I didn't figure out soon enough to keep something else from happening."

I grimaced. "Okay. The best we all can do is keep trying to find more answers."

"Listen, I have to go," Stanton said.

We walked back to the vehicles. Stanton loaded Gus and the stakes in his car and said good-bye to the kids. The ride back to the inn was filled with happy chatter from Tommy and Allie, while my mind whirled from this new situation. I parked next to Daniel's bus, and we all got out. He was tinkering with the engine but straightened up and turned to me when

I approached him. His welcoming smile disappeared when he saw the look on my face.

"Daniel and I have some business to talk about," I said to Tommy and Allie. "Why don't you two go in and get some milk and cookies?"

Tommy's face broke into a wide grin. "Mom made chocolate chip ones today. Come on, Allie. I'll race you."

The two sprinted for the back door, Fred right behind them.

"What happened?" Daniel asked.

I told him.

"Whoa," Daniel said. "What's going on around here?"

"I don't know, but I want to get over to the marina as soon as I can to see what I can find out. This is going to be a real blow to Rudy and Ivan. And they'll be questioned again. The more I can learn, the better."

I went into the inn. The kids were munching on their treats in front of the television.

I joined Helen where she was working at the counter. "Helen, let's go into the conference room. I need to talk to you."

Once there, I told her what had happened and that I needed to go to the marina. From there, I'd try to find the Doblinsky brothers. Once again, I needed her to take responsibility for the evening.

"When this is over, I'll pay you back in time."

"No worries, Kelly. It's not a problem for me, and what you're doing is important. I just hope whoever's behind this is found soon."

"Me, too."

She left, and I texted the Professor about what had happened and asked him to let Gertie and Mary know, but not the brothers. I wanted to tell them myself. The ride to the marina was short. A crowd of people had gathered off to one side. Three police cars and a coroner's van filled the lot. I spied a space at the end of a row, parked, and walked to the bait shop.

Joe saw me coming and gave a little wave. No happy expression on his face today. "It ain't lookin' good for the brothers."

"Have you seen them?"

"Not this afternoon. But I seen them this mornin'. Ivan threw the guy that was murdered off the boat. A bunch of us saw it. Stapleton had no business bein' on the *Nadia*, and we cheered Ivan on....Now that guy's been shot, the police will head for the boys sure as shootin'."

"Do you know when Rudy and Ivan left?

"Somewhere about ten."

"When did you last see Rick?"

"He stomped by me about nine thirty."

"Did you see him after that?"

"Nope. Had some customers. Busy with the weekend comin' up. Then fixed lunch. Didn't get back to my station until about one."

"Your station?"

"Sure. My lookout. Where I keep up with what's happenin'." He patted his chair.

"What time was the body discovered?"

"Guy came runnin' to use the phone around four thirty."

"Rudy and Ivan have an alibi for the afternoon. Let's hope they have one for the morning, if the police decide that was when he was shot," I said.

I stared off to where the *Nadia* was. Stanton's sturdy frame loomed over a shorter officer. Gus sat at his side. I saw him put what appeared to be a shirt to the dog's nose. Gus put his head down and began to cast from side to side.

"Joe, I think Stanton is having the bloodhound track Rick."

The officer and dog passed by us about six feet away and continued into the lot. Stanton didn't look in my direction.

"I'm going to follow them."

"Wait up, girl. You should take these."

Joe reached into a canvas bag next to his chair and pulled out a pair of binoculars.

He didn't strike me as a bird-watcher. What was he using them for? Was he spying on people?

"Joe? Really? Binoculars?"

"Now don't go gettin' any crazy ideas. I don't look through no windows. Don't like to move much with my arthritis and all. I can keep in the loop with these things."

I took them and hung them around my neck. "Thanks. I'll let you know what happens."

I hurried after Gus and Stanton but kept a good distance behind them. They went into a brushy, wooded area bordering the parking lot. I made my way down a barely discernable track, glad I hadn't changed out of my hiking boots. Branches with thorns grabbed at my ankles as I walked over thick trail debris.

I waded deeper and deeper into the brush, barely keeping them in sight. Then the foliage began to thin a bit, and I entered a small clearing. Stanton and Gus were on the far side. Stanton was bending down. I put the binoculars up to my eyes, adjusted the focus, and the officer leaped into view.

He was kneeling in front of a light green tent that had been tucked back into a brushy area. Outside was a fire pit with a metal grate over it. I assumed this was Rick's hideaway. It looked like no one needed or wanted a professional houseguest at the moment.

No wonder the empty boat lured him out. With the police done with their searching and the yellow tape in place, he must have figured he was safe from any visitors for a while, especially if he mostly used it at night.

The tent's flap was pulled back, and I saw an upside-down cot tucked on one side against the wall. A cooler at the back was on its side, its contents covering the canvas floor. I could make out a package of hot dogs and a brick of cheese.

As I surveyed the scene, I realized clothes had been strewn about outside. They didn't seem to be arranged for drying purposes; they were more like scattered about. An unzipped sleeping bag was crumpled in a ball outside the tent. The place looked like it had been ransacked. Was this the result of someone's fit of anger, or had the place been searched?

Stanton took a walkie-talkie off his belt and spoke into it. I remembered there was no cell phone service here. A short while later, I heard branches snapping behind me and stepped to one side as two officers strode by. One of them had a camera, and he began taking pictures of the scene.

I didn't think there'd be anything more to learn here. I made my way back to the marina, where Joe was holding down his fort. He was waiting, fingers laced together, his hands resting on his stomach.

I took off the binoculars and handed them to him. "Thanks. Good thinking about my taking them. They were a big help."

He looked at me expectantly. "What did ya learn?"

"It appears Rick had been camping in the woods. A warm boat with a stove and a refrigerator must've seemed mighty appealing."

Joe nodded. "Over the years, he probably got the code to the gate, as well as the showers and the bathrooms. He's done odd jobs for lots of people around here."

I sighed. "Makes sense he'd camp nearby when he didn't have a house to crash in."

I said good-bye and headed out. It was growing dark, and I was thankful for the marina lights. Swarms of bugs appeared to enjoy them as well as I glanced up and saw a dancing black cloud. I dug my keys out of my pocket and headed to the Doblinsky brothers' house.

Did they know yet? I'd soon find out.

I pulled into their driveway and an automatic light came on. I walked up the path to their house and knocked. Rudy opened the door partway.

"Kelly, welcome. Just a minute." A chain rattled as he closed the door, and then he opened it wide. "We don't get unexpected visitors at night very often, so we keep it chained."

"I understand. You're pretty remote here."

"Come in. Come in. We're just finishing dinner. Please join us."

I didn't realize how hungry I was until the rich aroma of their dinner hit me as I entered the kitchen.

"Beef stew." Ivan ladled some into a bowl. "Carrots, potatoes, onions, celery root—all good for you."

"Ivan uses an old family recipe from Russia. It's called zharkoye."

"No, really, I don't want to intrude." My stomach growled a loud *yes*.

"Always make plenty." Ivan put down the steaming bowl, along with some silverware.

"Okay. Thanks." I sat at the place he'd made for me.

"What brings you here?" Rudy asked.

"A couple of things I wanted to talk to you about."

I wasn't ready to dive into the murder yet. I wanted to break it as gently as possible, not just blurt it out. I figured I had a little time before the police got here.

"Eat first, then talk," Ivan said.

From the relaxed looks on their faces and the conversation about stew, I guessed they hadn't heard what had happened. I took a bite and savored the combination of carrots and beef in a rich sauce. A chunk of potato followed. They finished their bowls and stood.

My mother's voice came to me as I filled my soup spoon again. Something about not bolting my food. When I'd been out riding fence all day on the ranch, my manners sometimes went out the door at dinnertime.

I put down the spoon and sipped the tea Ivan had made while I'd been eating. Rudy was at the sink, rinsing their dishes.

Ivan stood next to a large pot on the stove. "Kelly, you like more?"

"No, thanks. I'm full. It was delicious."

Ivan nodded and turned off the burner. Rudy took my bowl and put it with the others. The brothers sat and looked at me expectantly. The phone rang in the other room. Rudy stood to answer it.

"Rudy, wait. Let the machine get it," I said.

He looked at me quizzically.

It might be the police, and I didn't want them to learn what had happened from them. "Please sit down."

He did as I asked.

"Ivan, you know the man you threw off the boat this morning? Rick Stapleton?"

He frowned and nodded.

"He's been murdered. Shot." I took a deep breath. "His body was found on the *Nadia*."

Chapter 22

Fear filled their faces.

"It...it can't be," Rudy said.

"I'm sorry, but it is. I asked you not to answer the phone in case it was the police. I wanted to be the one to tell you."

"Alive when we last saw him," Ivan rumbled.

"When was Rick murdered?" Rudy asked.

"They don't have an exact time of death yet. Joe at the bait shop saw him at nine thirty and the police were called at four thirty. I know you were at the meeting in the afternoon. Where were you in the morning?"

"We came home, had lunch, and then went to your inn."

"No alibi then?"

They both shook their heads.

"That would've made life simple, which usually isn't how it works," I said. "Maybe they'll find out he was killed when the Silver Sentinels were meeting and then you'll be covered."

"Will I be arrested?" Ivan's hands were balled into fists.

"Why do you think you would be?" I asked him in a gentle voice.

"I throw him off boat," he replied.

"You had every right to do that. He was trespassing. That doesn't mean you killed him. And remember, he was shot."

His hands unclenched a fraction, but deep frown lines remained.

"What happens now?" Rudy asked.

"At some point, I'm sure the police will question you. You tell them the truth."

A loud knock on the door interrupted us. I suspected the time for questions was upon us.

Rudy left and returned with Stanton. The officer's face was drawn, and his lips clamped together. A hint of cold night air trailed in after him.

Stanton frowned. "Office called and said they couldn't get in touch with anyone here. Said they left a message. I was planning to come by later but came now to be sure everything was okay, which it appears to be. Why didn't you answer the phone? You had me worried." His tone sounded sharp.

"I asked them not to," I said. "I wanted to be the one to tell them about Rick's murder and the involvement of their boat. I did that right before you arrived."

Stanton seemed to relax a bit, and he gave a tired smile. "Okay. I understand." He looked at Rudy and Ivan. "I need to ask you some questions."

Ivan had stood during our conversation, turned on the stove, and was stirring the stew. "Deputy Stanton, you eat and ask."

"Thanks, Ivan, I'll pass. I'll get something later."

I figured he hadn't had time to get anything to eat. Knowing how hungry I was, he must have been famished.

I looked at Stanton. "It's beef stew and it's really good. The food gave me energy that wasn't there when I walked through the door a little while ago."

I could see him hesitate.

"Tell you what: Let's get the questions out of the way first, then I'll take you up on your offer." He took off his gray Stetson and his heavy police coat.

Rudy said, "There's a rack by the back door."

Most of the pegs had been covered with wool hats and heavy sweaters, but a few were empty. Stanton deposited his hat and jacket and joined us at the table. He took out his notepad and a pen.

"Would you like something to drink?" Rudy asked.

"Water would be nice," Stanton answered.

Ivan placed a glass on the table in front of the officer.

"Well," he said, sounding weary. "As Kelly has now told you, Rick Stapleton's been killed and his body was found on your boat. Tell me what happened this morning."

Rudy nodded. "We received a call from the police department that we were clear to return to the boat. Ivan and I caught the bus after breakfast and went to the marina.

Ivan sat down next to his brother, across the table from the officer.

"Ivan checked the deck to see if everything was in order while I entered the boat. I climbed down the ladder and saw an unfamiliar jacket on the dining room seat. I thought maybe one of the police officers had left it there so didn't really think anything of it. I turned the corner into the hallway, intending to check the back room. I ran right into Rick, and he took a swing at me."

"I hear yell and go down into boat," Ivan said.

Rudy continued, "Rick said, 'Sorry, man, you surprised me.'"

"I don't think he was going after you personally...more of a knee-jerk reaction," Stanton remarked.

"Yes, that's what I think," Rudy said.

"Sounds like he was real edgy," Stanton added.

Rudy nodded. "He kept fidgeting and explaining he had nowhere to stay, the boat was empty, sorry if he caused a problem…"

I joined in. "What you're describing sounds like nonstop rambling."

"I stop it," Ivan said. "Tell him get off boat now. He began talking again. I grab arm and push toward ladder."

Rudy took over. "Rick went up a couple of steps, then started to turn, as if to come back down. Ivan shoved him hard. Rick's head hit one of the rungs. I suspect it hurt, considering the strength of Ivan's push."

"Yah. I follow him up to deck, then take back of shirt in my right hand, belt in left, and throw him onto the dock."

"He yelled about his jacket," Rudy said. "I got it and tossed it to him. He left and that was the last we saw of him."

"Found a few of his shirts on boat," Ivan added.

"We put them in a paper bag and put his name on it, planning to give them back to him when we found out where he was," Rudy said.

"I saw the clothes," Stanton said. "I used one of the shirts to get a bloodhound to track him."

"I talked to Joe," I said. "He told me people witnessed what happened on the dock and said Rick passed by him around nine thirty."

Stanton nodded. "We interviewed a number of people, and they were all on the same page about the incident and seeing Rick leave. Tell me what you did for the rest of the day."

Rudy and Ivan shared with Stanton what they'd told me about their activities.

"With the way Rick's camp was torn apart, I think it was searched." Stanton pulled out his phone, touched the face of it a couple of times, then turned it so the brothers could see what was on the screen.

I rose and went to stand behind them. Stanton's photo showed the inside of the boat. Cushions from the dining room set were upended, and the sleeping area curtains were pulled back. Blankets were piled on the floor. Stanton scrolled to another photo. Contents of the kitchen drawers littered the floor, as if someone had pulled them out and upended them.

From the stunned expressions on the Doblinsky brothers' faces, the chaos was a surprise to them.

"Did it look like this when you left?" Stanton asked.

Rudy looked shocked. "N…n…no." He had trouble getting the word out.

Stanton put down his phone. "The man in charge of the search texted and said that while it's a mess, nothing has been destroyed. It doesn't seem like a personal vendetta or vandalism. I'm guessing whoever did it wanted to find something Rick had." He turned to me. "Quite likely it's that gold coin we've talked about."

Stanton closed his notepad. "The stew smells delicious. I'd like to take you up on your offer of having some. Dinner hasn't happened yet today."

Ivan pulled a bowl and plate from the cupboard. "Happy to. You help us. Need to let us do same for you. Is fair." After filling the bowl, he placed it in front of the deputy sheriff, then pushed a platter of French bread and a tub of butter in his direction. "Go good with stew."

Stanton took a slice, buttered it, and bit into the thick bread.

I could almost hear his stomach say, *At last.*

Stanton looked at his notes while eating his dinner at a leisurely pace. He was doing a better job than I had done in terms of dining decorum. The brothers straightened the kitchen while I checked my phone for messages.

"What happens now?" I asked after a few minutes.

"Officers are working their way through the *Nadia* as we speak."

Stanton sat back and pushed his now-empty bowl to one side. Ivan took it and filled it again without asking. The two men were of comparable size, and Ivan must have felt the officer could eat more.

Stanton's phone emitted a sound. He picked it up and checked the screen. "They found the coin. Rick had taped it to the bottom of one of the credenza drawers in the bedroom. Anyone doing a quick search would be hard-pressed to find it. He planted it at the very back."

"Why didn't he hide it in the woods near where he was staying?" I asked.

Stanton shook his head. "The coin is worth a lot of money, and I'm guessing he wanted it with him wherever he was."

"Makes sense," I said.

"They're sending me a photo. Rudy, will you know if the coin is one you sold to Alexander?"

"Maybe," he replied. "I'll definitely know if it's not one of mine. I kept photos as well as the ledger you've seen. If it matches one of my sales, the next question would be was it mine or Clay's. Our money came from the same source. And, though it's unlikely, it could have been sold by someone else."

"Process of elimination can be very useful," Stanton said.

His phone pinged again. I was still standing behind the brothers. As he passed the phone to Rudy, I saw a gold coin with the year *1897* imprinted on it and the number *50*. It had the image of a man's head in the center. A second photo had an emblem of some sort.

"Is fifty rubles," Ivan said.

"Nicholas the second," Rudy added. "The other picture is the royal family coat of arms." Rudy rose and put the phone on the table. "I'll go get my information."

Stanton finished his second bowl of stew. "Thanks, Ivan. That hit the spot." He turned to me. "You were right. I feel much better."

Remembering the lengthy trip to the basement, I knew it would be a while before Rudy returned. "Deputy Stanton, two men have been shot, but no one heard anything. What gives with that? People live at the marina. Do you think they were shot somewhere else and brought to the boat?"

He raised his eyebrows and gave me one of his looks that said *you know I can't tell you anything.*

"We have nothing to share publicly yet." He paused, and his face softened a bit. "As you're guessing, one possibility is they were killed elsewhere. You've probably watched enough television you can figure out what another explanation might be."

I thought for a moment. "A silencer on the gun?"

The officer nodded. "That's how a person can get shot with people nearby and no one hears anything."

"That's pretty high-tech, isn't it?"

He shook his head. "It's a piece of equipment. Unfortunately, guns and gun-related items are easy to buy if you know the right people."

Rudy returned with his sales book. "I have two lists. One I have the date of sale, what was sold, and how much money I received. The other one is my description of the coins in order of their worth. I have been selling them for many years, so being able to look it up by fifty rubles will save a lot of time."

"Good to know, Rudy," Stanton said. "That might be helpful at some later point."

Rudy flipped through a few pages and ran his finger down a neatly written list. "Not mine. You'll need to check with Clay."

"Okay. I'll do that." Stanton picked up his phone and put it in his pocket.

He sat back and rubbed his hand over his face. My dad did that at the end of particularly long days.

Stanton looked at the brothers. "Rudy and Ivan, I know all of this is difficult for you. I don't know what's going on, but I don't believe you're guilty of anything. Just want you to know that. You and the Silver Sentinels have done a lot for this community. I'll do everything I can to get to the bottom of these murders as fast as possible."

Gruff as he could be at times, I knew Stanton was fond of his crime-solving seniors.

"Thank you, Deputy Sheriff," Rudy said.

Ivan nodded. "Yah."

"Do you know yet when Rick died?" I asked.

"They still don't have a definitive time of death. The first officers on the scene suspect he hadn't been killed right before they got there, given how the body felt. We have reports of Rick being spotted around eleven in the parking lot headed toward the boats. We're thinking between then and early afternoon."

Then it hit me. I blinked rapidly a few times and felt queasy. It must've shown.

Stanton frowned. "Is something wrong?"

I took in a deep breath. "I stopped to talk to Joe on my way home from seeing Tom and Harvey. I was there between those times."

Stanton had opened his notepad. "Did you see anything that might be connected?"

I shook my head and shared with him my conversation with Joe.

Stanton closed his notepad and stood. "I need to get the dog home and feed him. I have a long night ahead."

He got his things and said good-bye. Rudy walked him to the door.

I felt rooted to my chair. I shuddered. Rick might have been murdered as I was talking with Joe. His body could've been there the whole time. The killer or killers could've walked past me.

Murder was hitting close to home.

Chapter 23

I unglued myself from the chair seat and helped Ivan wash the dishes. "Are you still going to the festival?"

He wiped a bowl with a dishcloth. "Yah. Sure. Maybe find out something."

Rudy had returned as I asked the question. "Hiding won't bring answers. Being here by ourselves didn't keep us out of the investigation into Rick's death."

"True," I said.

We promised to look for one another tomorrow. Rudy followed me to the door and kept watch as I got into my Jeep. There was no being too careful with all that was happening.

* * * *

The next morning, after the breakfast chores were done, I changed clothes for the event. I'd noticed the thick grass when I delivered the baklava and decided lightweight hiking boots would be a good choice. Black jeans and a green sweater finished my attire.

I'd wear the navy fleece Michael Corrigan had given me when he offered me the job. Embroidered on it was *Manager* with *Redwood Cove Bed and Breakfast* under it. No reason not to do a little advertising.

When I entered the kitchen, Tommy, Helen, and Fred were there. Tommy was finishing his breakfast. Fred nudged his empty bowl, pushing it around the floor. He was probably hoping for more kibble to magically appear.

"Looks like you're ready for the festival," Helen said.

"The Cossacks ride early and I don't want to miss them."

"We're going to watch them in the afternoon," Helen said. "Tommy and Allie want to start with the horse-drawn wagon ride."

"Yeah," Tommy said. "I've never been on one. Neither has Allie."

"I think you're smart to do it early. The lines could get long as the day progresses. I understand the wagon goes around the whole festival, and it's like a guided tour to the different activities."

Helen nodded. "That's what it sounded like to me, too. Daniel and I are going to go along with the kids and plan the day as we learn about what's being offered."

"I'll take care of the wine and appetizers tonight. You have the evening off after all the extra work you've been doing."

"Thanks, Kelly."

Tommy held up what looked like a plastic box. "Mom bought this for Fred to play with in his dog run while we're gone."

I went over and looked at it. I'd seen similar ones in the past and knew it was a dog puzzle. Treats were put in it, and the dog had to figure out how to get them out. It would keep Fred well occupied.

I took off my fleece from one of the pegs at the back door. "I'm sure we'll run into one another. See you later."

The drive to the festival was short. A steady stream of cars entered the grassy field being used as a parking lot, but there was still plenty of room. An auxiliary lot had been decided upon and shuttles would run when this area was full. I parked a couple of rows from the front and headed for where the activities were being held.

The road leading to the clearing had been blocked off with sawhorses. Ticket sellers stood at the gaps between the barriers. A sign said only residents and their guests could drive through. I joined the lines to buy my ticket and get a program.

When that was done, I walked down the narrow country road, charming inns on my left, the field nearly full of brightly clad performers on my right. Redwood forest encircled the area, creating a magnificent backdrop.

I stopped at one inn to admire a particularly attractive sign. I'd have to replace ours soon. I took out my phone and photographed it. The name *Bellington Bed and Breakfast* sounded familiar; then I remembered that was where some committee members were staying.

"Can I help you?"

Startled, I looked around. There was a voice but no person.

"Up here."

On a second-floor balcony, I spied her—a heavyset woman with short brown hair and wearing an apron covered with flowers.

"Hi. I was just admiring your sign. Who made it?" I asked.

"Just a sec. I'll come down."

A few minutes later, the stout woman emerged and came down the walkway. "A local woodworker." She glanced at the corner of my fleece. "You must be the new manager at Redwood Cove B and B."

"I am."

"Maude Upton." She shoved a hand in my direction.

"Kelly Jackson."

We shook hands.

"I'll call your place and leave his contact information," Maude volunteered.

"Thanks." I pulled one of my cards from my purse and handed it to her.

"He's reliable and dedicated to doing a good job. He does more than signs. You might be able to use him for other projects."

I saw a couple of comfortable-looking rocking chairs on the porch. "Looks like you have a front-row seat for some of the activities."

"I do indeed. I've been enjoying watching them practice the last few days. Would you like to join me?"

"No, thanks. I'm meeting a friend."

She reached in an apron pocket, pulled out a card, and handed it to me. "If you have any questions I might be able to help with, please give me a call."

"Will do."

I looked at the map of the festival I'd printed. The Cossacks performed at the far end, where temporary bleachers had been assembled. The festival had been blessed with a sunny morning, not the more common fog. The sunrays through the trees created a dappled road of shadows and light.

Thoughts of Rick entered my mind as I walked, and I pushed them away. Not now. Not here. *Let it go.* My mind needed some peace right now.

I arrived at the stands. In front of them, an area had been roped off, creating a large ring. Off to one side, several chestnut-colored horses stood, held by men dressed in tan britches and black military-style jackets. They wore tall black riding boots and the classic Cossack woolen hats I'd seen in photographs.

I didn't see Scott. Then I felt a tap on my shoulder. I turned, and my gaze met his blue eyes. For a moment, my heart quickened. Then I looked away, my usual relationship-stopping tactic.

"Ready for our date?"

I could tell by the twinkle in his eyes and the mischievous smile, he was having fun teasing me.

"Where do you want to sit?" he asked.

"Let's go up a few rows so we can see the riders all the way around the ring."

We were early and had no trouble finding a space. I was curious about Scott's feelings toward Alena. She was like him—a city person. Had there been a kinship there when they'd met?

I settled myself on the hard bench. "I hear there's going to be a formal Russian ball at the Community Center. Where's it going to be held? I didn't think the center had an area big enough for that."

"Michael decided he wanted to build a large multipurpose area. It's beyond the gymnasium. You haven't been to that area of the grounds. I'll show you the next time you come. It's not done yet but will be in time for the dance."

"The building sounds like another one of Michael's good ideas."

"It's working out really well for the veterans. Some of them wanted to learn the carpentry trade, so Michael arranged for them to get training at the same time." Scott shifted on the seat next to me. "How did you hear about the ball?"

"Alena Stepanova came by to make arrangements to use the conference room again. She mentioned it."

"Ah, yes, Alena."

What did that mean? "You two probably struck it off really well. I know city life is what you prefer."

A hint of a smile showed on his face. "We talked about some restaurants and the San Francisco scene."

"I think she'd like to get to know you better than someone she's doing business with. She asked if we were dating."

"And we are."

"Scott, I don't consider this dating. I like to think of this as two friends doing something together."

He took my hand. "Kelly, I'm just giving you a hard time. I know you're still finding your way after your divorce." He looked at my fingers. "If it helps any, I prefer short nails with clear polish to crimson Dracula nails that look like lacquered weapons."

I didn't think fashion-conscious Alena would appreciate the comparison to a vampire, but I didn't care.

"Besides, I'm beginning to like it here…and I'd miss my llamas."

I could feel a blush start and was saved by the Cossacks. I focused on the riders as they did a full-tilt run around the arena. The stands vibrated. They came to a sliding stop in front of the bleachers. The men and horses were still. A bell began to ring. I consulted my program and saw that a bell ringing would signal the start of the festival.

When the ringing concluded, an announcer came over the loudspeaker. "Welcome, everyone. You are about to see unparalleled horsemanship skills. We are honored to have with us today six Cossacks and their magnificent steeds."

One man with a long, dark mustache urged his horse forward out of the line. He held a long black whip like I'd seen in Rudy's basement. He gave a yell, and the horse jumped into a full gallop. The man stood in his stirrups and waved the whip in a circle over his head, then on one side of the horse, and then on the other. They did one ride around the ring with this maneuver.

As the Cossack approached the stands, he flipped the whip from side to side, creating a cracking sound. I remembered what Ivan had told me about them using the whip against attacking wolves. I could see how that could be done with his whip-wielding skills.

I never saw the horse flinch. If he'd been flicked with the black leather instrument, he would've reacted.

The next Cossack came forward. He started to lope around the ring, then suddenly, he swung to the side like he was about to fall off. The next thing I knew, he was back in the saddle, but now he held a sword. It had been on the ground, and he had picked it up. Several other items had been planted in the ring, all of which he successfully retrieved.

Each time he appeared to fall, the crowd gasped. Each time he was back in the saddle, they cheered. For him to be able to do what he did required a highly trained horse with an even, smooth pace and a strong individual.

The hour passed quickly. One team had a person leap from their horse to the back of another horse, landing behind the rider. The now-unmanned horse stayed next to the horse with two riders. After several minutes, the rider jumped back onto his own mount. Another demonstrated masterful lance skills. Each Cossack had his own specialty.

For a finale, all the riders raced around the ring, standing on their saddles. The crowd burst into applause. I clapped and clapped. I'd definitely be back for the afternoon performance.

I turned to Scott, adrenaline coursing through me. "What did you think?"

"Unbelievable. Can you ride like that?"

I burst out laughing. "No way."

"Just thought I'd ask. One time you mentioned maybe going riding together one day, and I wanted to know what I might be getting in to."

"For your first time out, a nice quiet walk, I assure you."

We descended from the stands and made our way through the crowd. Demonstrations and performing groups had been given places around the perimeter of the large field. Music filled the air. In the center, a food court had been set up.

"What do you want to see next?" he asked.

"I hadn't marked anything else in particular on the program except for the Cossacks. I want to see them again this afternoon."

"Let's work our way around and see what strikes us."

We walked side by side, stopping when a display interested us or when we wanted to hear more from a particular singing group. I spotted Clay observing a candle-making demonstration.

I gestured toward him. "There's Clay Johnson, one of the relatives Rudy recently met."

I got Scott up to speed on what had happened. We walked over to Clay, and I made the introductions.

"Are Timur and Verushka here?" I asked.

Clay shook his head. "They grew up spending most of their life hiding. As adults, they continue to prefer to keep their distance from others. Besides, Mother's been getting ready for the tea. It's been years since I've seen her do so much cooking. She's really excited."

"I'm looking forward to it," I said.

Clay frowned. "Bad news about Rick Stapleton being murdered and Rudy and Ivan being pulled into it because he was found on their boat."

"What happened?" Scott asked.

I told him in a few short sentences, leaving out the part about me following Stanton.

"That matches what I heard," Clay said. "I stopped by to see Harvey Goldstein. Had a coin I wanted to get an estimate on, and he told me about the murder."

"Did the police contact you about the coin they found?" I asked.

"They did," Clay said. "It matched the description of one I sold to Alexander a few days before he died."

"Was Rick working there at the time?" I asked.

"Yes. Alexander complained and complained about Rick and said he was close to firing him."

I believed we had one of our answers. It was highly unlikely an unhappy employer would give an expensive coin to a disliked employee. The chances of that were about nil.

I was ready to assume Rick had stolen it.

It probably had been caught on camera.

Was that why he was murdered?

Chapter 24

Scott and I said good-bye to Clay and continued our circuit of the events, my mind still on the question the discussion with Clay had brought up. A wagon approached, pulled by two classic Clydesdales. Their long ebony manes and tails provided a striking contrast to their glistening reddish-brown coat. Both had white blazes and fetlocks. Tommy and Allie, seated in the front, shouted a hello as they passed. Daniel and Helen occupied the seat behind them and waved a greeting. Scott and I waved back.

We meandered for another half hour. Then we headed for the food court and shared a lunch of piroshki and beef stroganoff.

I checked my watch. "It's about time for the Cossacks to ride again. Do you want to come with me?"

"I need to get back to the center. The contractor in charge of building the new rooms is coming by this afternoon to check on the progress. He had to go out of town for a couple of days at the end of last week. Normally, he wouldn't be by on a Saturday."

"Okay."

"I've enjoyed this…and a chance for us to have a pleasant stroll together."

Our gazes met.

"I enjoyed it, too." I looked away, breaking the connection. "Glad to hear the llamas are growing on you and are becoming friends."

"They're excellent listeners, and they must have accepted me. I haven't been spit on once."

I shot a quick glance at him and was rewarded by one of his mischievous grins.

"Come by next week and I'll show you the new building…and you can talk to your llama."

"I'll give you a call to set up a time," I said.

With that, we went our separate ways. I felt myself inching closer and closer to a relationship with him…but slow worked fine for me right now.

I enjoyed the Cossacks as much the second time, if not even more than the first. I knew what was coming and concentrated on watching how they did each of the stunts. After their whirlwind galloping finale, they headed for the barnlike structure where I'd delivered the baklava and talked with Vladimir. Wanting to see the horses up close and check out their saddles, if possible, I walked in that direction.

When I reached the building, I didn't see any sign of the horses or the men. I walked around a corner of the converted barn and immediately spun back around and retreated in the direction I'd come as quickly as possible.

I'd stumbled on Vladimir and Alena in a passionate kiss. I didn't think they'd seen me. I was glad she had her claws in him and not Scott.

I went around the other side of the building and to the back, where I found a long horse trailer and the horses tied to it. Parked next to it was a house trailer. Two crewmembers emerged and walked past me.

I recognized the one with the shaved head who had approached Vladimir during the food delivery. The other one sported a crew cut and had snake tattoos covering both arms. I remembered Tom saying one of the organizers was bringing a team from San Francisco. I wondered who it was. It didn't seem relevant to our investigation, but I'd ask anyway when I got a chance. You never knew when a piece of information would prove useful.

The Cossacks weren't in sight. I walked over but didn't approach the horses. I'd want to ask permission for that. Their muscular hindquarters and stocky build reminded me of the American Quarter Horses we raised on the ranch. As I was admiring them, one of the riders came from around the back of the trailer. He was young and slender, with dark brown hair.

"Hi! I was just admiring your horses. What breed are they?"

He smiled at me. "Russian Dons. They originated in the steppes of Russia where the Don River flows, hence their name. I'm Yaro, by the way."

"I'm Kelly Jackson. I really enjoyed your performance. You and the others were amazing."

"Thanks." He pulled off his turbanlike hat. "My *papakha* is too warm for a California afternoon."

He pulled a handkerchief from his pocket and wiped his brow. The saddles had been placed next to the back of the horse carrier. They had loops and handles sewn in at a variety of places. One of them had a short metal pole in place of a saddle horn.

Yaro noticed me examining them. "Would you like me to explain how we do the tricks and what the different pieces on the saddle are?"

"Yes. Very much so. I barrel race, but I've never done any trick riding."

"I've seen that type of racing at rodeos. You are a very skilled rider to be able to stay on with all the turns the horse does while running as fast as it can."

"Thanks."

Yaro explained that each rider had a custom saddle designed to help them perform their stunts. He showed me how the different straps were used and how to properly grip them.

"Stop by tomorrow if you get a chance," he said. "A number of the performers, including our team, are staying over for a couple of days to get in some extra practice."

I thanked him and was headed back to the event area when my phone rang. This time I recognized the unusual number ending in three sevens.

"Hi, Joe. What's happening?"

"Got news. Not real important, but wanted you to know. Turns out one of my friends spotted Rick on the dock yesterday mornin' at eleven. I didn't see him because he used the entrance at the far end of the parkin' lot."

I knew this from Stanton but didn't want Joe to feel unappreciated, so I didn't mention it. "Thanks. That gives us more information about the time of death."

"That's what I was thinkin'."

"Late morning, or very early afternoon is what the police are guessing. You know, Joe, it's possible he was killed while we were talking."

No response. Only silence.

"Joe, are you still there?"

"Just thinkin' about what you said. Don't like that idea."

I heard him sigh.

"Why didn't we hear shots?" he asked.

I decided I'd do what Stanton had done to me. "You're the crime scene reporter. How does someone show up murdered with no one hearing the shots?"

"Person killed somewhere else and the body dumped," Joe replied. "Unlikely to be the case here. Hard to go unnoticed."

"And how else? Think about TV cop shows."

"In the crime shows, sometimes there are silencers," he said.

"Right. The police haven't said anything for sure yet, but that's what I'm thinking."

"Well, if I hear anythin' else, I'll let you know."

"Thanks."

I mingled with the crowd, stopping to listen to a chorus. They sang a verse in Russian, then did the same one again in English. The song told of the struggles of a family during a snowy winter many years ago. A good fit for a Russian heritage festival.

I saw Allie and Tommy amid a group of dancers. From the repetitive movements, I guessed their partners were teaching them the steps to the folk dance the musicians were playing.

Tom Brodsky joined me as I watched them. "Are you enjoying the festival?"

"Very much. I watched the Cossacks twice and spoke with one of the men. He explained how they do the different stunts and showed me the special saddles they use."

"They are always one of the most popular groups."

"I noticed a house trailer parked next to the horses. I remember you talking with Diane at the stable about borrowing it and one of the organizers requesting it. I'm curious. Who was that?"

"Alena Stepanova. The crew she brought are doing a great job. Hard workers. I hope we can get them next year."

Alena. Did the men have a secondary purpose? Were they bodyguards?

I wondered if Tom knew anything about Rick Stapleton that would be helpful. It was a big leap from Cossacks to murder. How to make that transition? Maybe the Russian connection.

I continued casually, "I haven't seen Rudy and Ivan Doblinsky yet. I know they said they were going to come." I sighed. "Maybe it felt like a bit too much, considering what happened on their boat."

Tom nodded. "I heard about Rick Stapleton getting killed. Unbelievable what's happening around here."

"Did you know Rick?"

"A bit. I hired him for odd jobs and at tax time. He was good at numbers, and when the big April crunch hit, he helped me out. Rick also was the go-between for me and Alexander."

"What do you mean?"

"I did the books for the store. Alexander and I wanted nothing to do with each other, so Rick brought the information to me."

My heart raced. "You did the books? You worked for the Williams Company?"

"Yes."

"Who owns it?" I asked.

"I don't know."

My excitement faded. "But…but if you worked for them, who did you communicate with?"

"I got calls from various secretaries. We never discussed who owned it."

My shoulders slumped.

"But if you want to know, Vladimir can probably tell you. His company is the one who arranged for the lease of the store."

Vladimir? How was he involved? Were we close to finding out who was behind the hidden cameras?

"Thanks for telling me. I'll check with him."

Tom and I parted company. My phone signaled a text message. It was the Professor, letting me know the group was meeting at the Russian Tea House in the food court. I told him I'd be there.

I was looking at the ground and thinking about what Tom had said when I almost ran into Alena. She wore a long red skirt and a loose, white peasant blouse. A wide, multicolored embroidered belt cinched at her waist, emphasizing her hourglass figure.

Her bright, red lipstick was perfect. Not a smudge to be seen. How could that be after what I'd seen?

"Hi, Kelly. How are you enjoying the festival?"

"It's a lot of fun. There certainly is a lot to see."

"Yes. The committee works all year to bring the different groups together."

"It's all so well organized. Very impressive."

"Thank you. I will pass on your kind words at our next meeting. I must go now. One of the groups has a question for me."

She walked toward one of the dance stages. I found the Sentinels seated at a table covered with a crocheted tablecloth like my grandmother used to make. Before joining them, I went to the counter and ordered an orange tea laced with hints of mint. I was handed a miniature teapot, the steam rising from it an aromatic blend of spices.

"Good timing." I joined the Sentinels. "I have news."

I proceeded to share what I'd learned from Clay and Tom. I didn't think the incident with Vladimir and Alena had any bearing on the murder investigations, so I left that out.

"Finally feels like some progress is being made." Mary pushed a plate of cookies into the middle of the table. "I bought these for us to share."

"I have some news as well," Gertie said. "I ran into Harvey's mother. He called and told her he had one of his gold customers back and was thrilled."

"Let's do a quick run-through of our suspects," the Professor said, "starting with Harvey."

Gertie nodded. "If Harvey killed Alexander to get his customers back, he's getting what he wanted."

"Do we know any reason he might have had for murdering Rick?" Rudy asked.

I sipped my tea. "I don't know of any, but Rick seemed to rub people the wrong way. We also don't know if the same person is responsible for both deaths."

"True," the Professor said. "Let's keep an open mind. Hopefully, the police will release the information about the bullets soon."

"Tom's on the list," Mary said. "We know where he stood with Alexander. He's doing the books for a business we think might be questionable because of how hard it's been to get information. Maybe Rick stumbled on something he shouldn't have seen. Tom might be involved in illegal activities, and Rick found out and Tom killed him."

"We need to remember Rick was a suspect in the murder of Alexander," the Professor said. "We can't rule him out for that murder."

"I wonder why the body was left out in the open where it could be seen," Gertie said.

Mary nibbled on a sugar cookie. "Maybe because of the fight people witnessed, the murderer thought Ivan would be considered a very likely suspect having the body found soon after their altercation."

"If they were both killed for stealing from the Williams Company," I said, "it could be a message to others that wasn't a smart thing for someone to do."

I glanced at the counter and saw Vladimir's broad-shouldered back. He was wearing a black sports coat and blue jeans.

"Vladimir's here," I whispered. "I'll see if I can get him to come over and introduce you to him."

Vladimir turned and surveyed the seating area. It was packed, but we had empty spaces at our table. I stood and waved to him. He walked over.

"Please join us," I said.

"Thanks," he replied and sat.

"I'd like you to meet some of my friends." I made the introductions.

They exchanged pleasantries and comments about the festival.

Time to ask questions. "I was talking with Tom Brodsky earlier," I said. "The Professor has been trying to reach the Williams Company that has the lease on Alexander Koskov's store. Tom said your corporation might be able to help with that because your business was involved in the paperwork."

The Professor chimed in. "I have a friend who might be interested in buying them out of their remaining months. I left a message but haven't heard anything. Do you know who the owner is and how to contact him or her?"

Bravo, Professor. So innocently asked.

I don't think I was the only one holding my breath as we waited for an answer.

"I do know the owner," Vladimir said. "Alena Stepanova's father, Boris Baranov."

Chapter 25

"Boris is very busy at the moment," Vladimir said.

Trying to get out of jail.

"Besides, his business manager is the one you would want to talk to. Boris doesn't handle specifics like leases. I'd be happy to talk to him for you."

"That would be splendid. Thank you for your help." The Professor reached inside his blazer and pulled out a slim black leather wallet. He extracted a card and handed it to Vladimir.

Vladimir slipped it into his coat pocket. "I'm glad to hear all of you are enjoying the festival. I'm going to check on the groups due to begin in the next session to see if they need anything. Nice meeting you all."

The group responded that they'd enjoyed meeting him as well.

As soon as he was out of earshot, the Professor said, "That finishes the research into ownership."

"It doesn't give us the answer to who's behind the cameras," I said. "Did Boris order them, or is the business manager doing something on his own?"

"Right, Kelly," Gertie said. "We also don't know if there is something criminal happening at the store. People involved in organized crime often have legitimate businesses."

"It does give us a new focus, however," the Professor said. "Rather than searching for who owns the business, perhaps we should learn more about the manager and who ordered the hidden cameras."

Mary picked up her teacup and took a sip. "Rudy, I think this is a good time for us to talk about what I discovered concerning your samovar."

The Professor, Gerti, and I looked at Rudy questioningly.

"First, let me give our friends the background behind your inquiries," Rudy responded.

The word *samovar* rang a bell, but I didn't remember what it was. "What is a samovar, Rudy?"

"It is a large Russian metal container used to make tea. The one Mary is referring to is an antique. The centerpiece holds fuel such as wood chips or coal. Those are ignited, and they heat water in the container."

"Thanks," I said.

"Our mother had one in Russia," Ivan said.

Rudy went on to tell us that when he was born, the prince had bought her a beautiful samovar. Rudy, Ivan, and their mother lived in a cottage the prince had built for them. He hadn't felt it was right for them to be living in the servants' quarters, and there were some people jealous of Tatiana. As the years passed, the prince routinely came over for tea and to visit with Rudy and Ivan.

"Yah," Ivan chimed in. "Rudy and I had fun gathering pine cones in the woods for fuel."

"Our mother was heartbroken when she had to leave it behind when we fled Russia," Rudy said. "The samovar was too heavy and cumbersome for us to carry. While it was very valuable, we had to take the smaller items instead."

"Rudy recently bought one," Mary said, "and asked me to check its provenance to see what more I could learn about it."

"It's not normally something I would buy," Rudy said. "But when I saw it in Alexander's shop, it brought back memories of my mother and father. I even wondered if it could be the one we left behind. I don't remember exactly what it looked like. I was young, and samovars weren't of interest to me. But...I thought maybe."

Mary continued, "What I've discovered is, the man Alexander said he bought it from has been dead for over a year. The receipt dates back to when the supposed seller was alive."

"What makes you use the word *supposed*, Mary?" the Professor asked.

"The samovar is made of silver and gold. It's a stunning piece of workmanship with detailed engravings. The makers put in identification marks to let people know they created it and also the year. The only one I can find so far that might be a match was stolen about six months ago from a high-end antique store."

"Interesting," Gertie said. "We still have the question of the mysterious boxes Rick told Daniel about on our charts."

Mary nodded. "I began to look into thefts of antiques. There have been a rash of similar crimes. All the stores carried high-end pieces. While they had security systems, they weren't the high-tech quality you'd find in a museum."

"You might be on to something," Rudy said. "How do we pursue gathering more information?"

I pulled out my phone and looked at the photos. "I took a picture of a couple of items in Alexander's shop I thought my mom might be interested in, as well as the information about them. Mary, I can send you what I have and you can research them." I paused. "I do think what you've discovered should be shared with Deputy Stanton. I know he's got two murders on his hands, but if Alexander was illegally importing stolen antiques, it might be connected to his death."

"I agree," Mary said. "I'll email him what I found out when I get home."

My phone pinged, notifying me of a text. "Speaking of Deputy Stanton, he said they just released the news that the same gun was used to kill Alexander and Rick."

"Ah..." the Professor said. "This day is bringing us a wealth of information."

"I believe this leads us to two possibilities," I said. "The same person killed both men or, if two different people did the shootings, they're connected in some way and sharing the gun."

Gertie nodded. "It's highly unlikely someone stole it from the person who killed Alexander and then used it to murder Rick. We can put it on our charts, but we'll keep it down at the bottom."

"Both Tom and Harvey knew Alexander and Rick," Mary said. "They could've worked together. They've lived in the area a long time, and it's highly likely they knew each other. They need to stay as suspects."

"Agreed," the Professor said. "And until we know more about who ordered the cameras, Boris stays on our chart, and we can add his business manager."

"I learned from Alena that Alexander had had a meeting with her father—all the more reason to contnue to treat him as a suspect," I said.

"I'd say we made progress today," Gertie said. "If I had my gavel, I'd hit the table and declare an end to the meeting."

The talk turned to the festival. From the smiles and happy chatter, I'd say we were all excited about what we had learned. Resolving the case and getting Ivan and Rudy out of harm's way would be a relief for all of us.

I confirmed my plans to pick the Doblinsky brothers up at nine o'clock in the morning for our visit to Timur, Verushka, and Clay. We'd pick up the items they'd inherited and partake of Verushka's Russian tea.

I returned to the inn and put out the appetizers and wine for the guests. I had an early dinner, cleaned up the dishes from the evening refreshments, read a bit, then called it a night, looking forward to tomorrow's adventure.

* * * *

The next morning, I picked up the brothers as planned. Rudy had his battered briefcase, which I suspected held his dagger and the case. The drive up the coast was no less harrowing than it had been the first time. The temporary traffic light was still in place at the landslide. It would be a while before the road was rebuilt, considering the extent of the damage.

I drove down the road in the grassy field surrounding the Russian mansion with its colorful turrets and parked in front as I had before. We got out, climbed the steps, and knocked on the door.

Timur answered. "Come in. Come in."

We followed him into the stately dining room, where Verushka gave us a warm welcome and Clay waved from his seat at the table. Two daggers rested on a mat on the table.

Clay rose. "Did you bring the case, Rudy? I've heard so much about the three daggers and the box made to house them. I'm excited to see it and the knives together."

Rudy placed his satchel on the floor. "I did."

He opened his bag and took out a cloth-wrapped item. Taking off the cover, he placed the silver case next to the daggers and opened it.

Rudy gestured to the case. "Timur, you please do the honors of bringing the family together."

Timur placed his dagger and Verushka's into the case alongside Rudy's.

Clay's eyes glittered. "The most valuable of the family treasures," he whispered.

He looked up, and I caught his eye. Clay quickly turned away.

They created a dazzling display of jewels. As a combined set with the detailed engraving on the case and the knives, I was sure what we were looking at was worth a fortune.

"It's good to have them together again," Timur said. "Even if it's only for a visit." He laughed.

"Now, we have much to show you," Verushka said. "We will do that first and have tea later."

"The prince and your mother always hoped they would find you," Timur said. "They built a room for the two of you to share as children."

"We haven't changed it," Verushka said.

Clay laughed quietly. "We have a lot of rooms, so we had no need."

As a group, we followed Timur and Verushka down the wide hallway. They stopped in front of a door, and Verushka opened it.

Timur turned to Rudy and Ivan. "Please. You enter first. It is your room."

They did as requested, and the rest of us joined them. Two single beds with ornate brocade covers occupied the room. A wooden nightstand stood between them. Two chests of drawers were against the wall opposite the ends of the beds. A portrait of what I knew to be the prince and their mother hung on the wall. An old leather traveling trunk rested next to one of the beds.

Timur pointed to it. "The items in there are yours. Your mother and the prince wanted you to have them if you were ever found."

The brothers sat on the bed. Rudy leaned forward, pulled back the metal clasp, and opened the trunk. A plain piece of material covered the items inside. Rudy pulled it back and revealed a highly decorated red military jacket. He gingerly removed it and held it up.

"That was the uniform our father wore when he married your mother." Tears formed in the corners of Verushka's eyes. "He was so proud and happy that day."

Rudy arranged the jacket carefully on the bed. Black pants followed. Underneath those was a fur cap with what appeared to be earflaps tied together at the top. Ivan picked it up and turned it gently in his hands.

"This is an *ushanka*. I used to put this on," Ivan said. "Was Father's. Pretended to talk to him after he died at sea."

Now I was beginning to tear up.

Timur handed them a notebook. "This is a diary your mother kept. She wrote to you on a daily basis. She said it kept you close to her and part of her life. There are more items in the case. Your mother told us she had written to you in the diary about the personal meaning to her of these objects."

Rudy opened it and read aloud. "'To my sons, Ivan and Rudy. How I hope we are reunited and I can be with you when you read my letters and notes to you. If that is not the case, then you will know you were always in my heart, and I will be watching you from heaven as you read how much I loved you.'"

Now the brothers had tears streaming down their cheeks.

"We will leave now. Give you some time to yourselves," Verushka said. "Tea is in an hour and a half. We will see you then."

Clay turned to me. "I mentioned showing you the grounds. Would you like me to do that?"

"Yes. Thanks."

We all left, and Clay led me to a door at the end of the hallway, and we went outside. First, we entered a flower garden with a winding stone path.

"Our grandmother started planting as many types of Russian flowers as she could find. Mother continues to care for them."

We wandered along, enveloped in their perfumed scent.

I stopped and sniffed one that looked like a daisy and was surprised by how sweet the smell was. "What's the name of this one?"

"Chamomile, a very common flower in Russia." Clay pointed to a small nearby building. "That was built first. The family lived there until the mansion was completed. I'll show it to you."

We walked toward it. Near the structure, there was another garden, this one more functional.

"It looks like you grow your own vegetables."

"We do," Clay said. "It saves us some money and provides fresh produce for our meals."

Entering the ground floor, I saw the Mercedes with the hood up and tools scattered on the ground next to it. I followed Clay up a flight of stairs, and he showed me the living quarters. Three bedrooms were on the second level. Tight quarters for grandparents, the prince and Tatiana, and young children. A third level had two small rooms and a kitchen where the servants had lived. We returned to the main level.

"We converted this part into a garage. I've been doing some repair work on the Mercedes. It's getting up there in years, but they can last a long time with proper maintenance. I made myself an office over here."

I followed him into a room with a desk, a swivel chair, and a computer. Posters and playbills covered the walls.

"It's nice to come out here and not have to think about being neat, which is the case in the main house."

One playbill was for *Hamlet*. "It looks like you enjoy the theatre."

"I do. What you see on the wall are from performances at the local high school. I helped the drama department put them on. I worked as a stage crew member."

Suddenly it hit me.

The fake blood on the dagger. Stanton had said it was like what was used in theatrical performances. On the walk and in the rooms upstairs, I had noticed some deferred maintenance in the form of rusty pipes and peeling paint. The comment about saving money with their own vegetables. Clay doing the mechanical work on the aging car.

I suspected the family was having financial issues.

Clay's desire to see the case and all the knives together. The look in his eyes when he referred to *the most valuable of the family treasures.*

It all added up.

I took a step backward to the open office door.

"You planted the knife on the boat to get to the case," I blurted out.

Chapter 26

Clay collapsed into the chair and buried his face in his hands. After a few moments, he straightened up and looked at me with weary eyes. "We're desperate for money. The family is on the verge of losing everything."

"Do Timur and Verushka know?"

"No. I didn't want to frighten them. There was nothing they could do to help." Clay sighed. "I found out about Rudy from Alexander. When I was selling him a coin, he commented on another Russian man with the same type of gold. I was shocked and wondered if it could be Rudy or Ivan. I knew about them from Timur and Mother. It didn't take me long to track them down. I saw the family resemblance in Rudy."

"But they said they hadn't met you," I said. "And why the elaborate ruse with the knife? Why not just talk to Rudy?"

"I didn't approach them. I needed to find out if Rudy had the case and, hopefully, still had his knife. He didn't know me. I was scared he wouldn't admit to having it. He might hide the case and keep it to himself." Clay's tone changed a bit and became stronger. "I was prepared to sue for the dagger box. The case belongs to the family."

"That still doesn't explain why you planted the dagger on the boat."

"I had to figure out a way to flush him out with the case. I thought he'd reveal his knife if the police questioned him, and maybe I'd be able to discover whether he had the case. The only way I could think to do that was with fake blood and an anonymous call to the police."

"Weren't you afraid someone would steal the dagger?"

"I rented a boat and kept watch on the *Nadia*. I almost had a heart attack when you showed up. I watched you search the deck, then walk away. I motored to the dock and kept my eye on you. When the police showed up, I felt the situation was back under control."

"How did you find out Rudy had the case and his dagger?"

Clay looked away, studying his papered walls. "I followed the three of you to the brothers' house. Those big windows with the view of the ocean are also good for seeing what's happening inside the home. Because it's on a knoll, it was easier for me to look in."

I shivered as I thought about him spying on us.

He looked at me pleadingly. "I know what I did was awful. I've never done anything like it before. When I said I was desperate, I meant it."

He seemed like a nice guy, and he clearly cared for his family. I wondered what I would have done in his place. How far would I go to keep my family from losing the ranch?

Desperate times call for desperate measures.

Clay continued, "When Rudy walked into the kitchen area, I slipped around the side to see in. As soon as I saw the case and the dagger, I left."

"It sounds like you had your bases covered."

Clay nodded. "I thought so. I figured the only risk was if someone at the police station took it. I felt I had no choice but to give it a try."

"Timur and Verushka need to know the situation, and you need to tell the others what you did."

"You're right." He shook his head. "I tried some investments over the years, but I wasn't good at it."

We returned to the dining room. The four others were there.

A large metal pot had been placed on the sideboard. I spotted ornate handles and engravings on the metal container. Various pastries lined the dining room table.

Verushka welcomed us. "The samovar is heating the water. We will be ready to begin soon."

Clay stood up straight and squared his shoulders. "I have something very important to share with all of you." He looked at Rudy. "And I have a question for you."

He told the story. It was a clever, well-thought-out plan. Other than the angst it had created for the brothers and the wasted police time, he hadn't done anything terrible. He might have an issue with the police when they found out.

Clay looked at Rudy. "Now, for my question. You know the circumstances we're in."

Rudy nodded.

"The case and the two daggers are worth a lot of money. However, I believe the entire set is worth millions. Are you willing to put your dagger and the case, along with Timur and Verushka's knives, if they're willing to part with theirs, up for sale?"

Rudy rose and put his hand on Clay's shoulder. "The case is not mine. It belongs to the family. I would gladly put my dagger with it to save this home. My grandparents built their piece of Russia in this place. My parents lived here." He smiled. "Ivan and I have a room here. This is the family home."

Relief flooded Clay's face. "Thank you. Thank you so much."

"Of course I'm willing to sell my dagger," Timur said. "I wish you had told us and not carried the burden alone."

Clay shrugged. "There wasn't anything you could do to help. Why make you worry?"

"We could sell furniture, artwork," Timur responded.

Clay shook his head. "That wouldn't give us the money we need to continue living here."

"You can have mine as well," Verushka said.

"We'll be able to save the property with the money the set will generate and put a nest egg aside." Clay addressed Rudy. "Whatever we get, you will receive a third."

Clay had mentioned he wasn't good with finances. I wondered how he planned on selling the case and knives.

"Clay, do you have any idea how you're going to go about selling the set?" I asked.

He shook his head. "Not really. Start contacting museums, I guess."

"I work for Resorts International. The owner, Michael Corrigan, is a wealthy, very savvy man with a lot of connections. With your permission, I'll get in touch with him to see if he's willing to help broker a deal. He knows Rudy and Ivan, and I'd be surprised if he didn't step in to help. He's that kind of person."

"Kelly, that would be great," Clay said. "I feel completely out of my league in this situation."

"I'll need your contact information, including a fax number. If he agrees to do it, I'm sure there'll be forms to fill out."

Clay nodded. "I'll get that for you before you leave."

"It is settled, then," Verushka said. "I hear the samovar singing. It's time for tea."

I'd been so engrossed in the discussion, I hadn't noticed the sounds being emitted from the tea set.

Rudy smiled. "Many Russians believe the samovar has a soul. In reality, it's the shape and acoustics of the container that causes the water to make peculiar noises when being brought to a boil."

Verushka had placed a delicate plate, teacup, and saucer out for each of us. Their red-and-green pattern emulated the turrets on the buildings. Tiny silver spoons had been placed on dark red cloth napkins. Jars of jam and honey had been put out, as well as a bowl of lemon slices. Verushka took my cup and filled it from the samovar and did the same for the others.

"Everyone, please eat. Enjoy!"

Enjoy we did indeed. The pastries were all melt-in-the-mouth quality. I detected the scent of cinnamon in the tea and a hint of orange.

I put my cup down. "Verushka, everything is delicious. Thank you so much for inviting me."

"You are very welcome. I searched out old family recipes I haven't made for years. It was fun, and I'd like to do it again in the not-too-distant future."

The men all chimed in with their words of appreciation. The maid I'd seen on the last trip cleared the dishes.

"We need to be going soon," I said. "What do you want to do with the dagger set?"

"I hadn't thought about that," Clay said. "We have a safe I can show you."

I followed him to the library, where he showed me an older model of a typical personal safe.

"Rudy has an actual vault. I believe it will be safer there. Besides, if my boss gets involved, it'll be easier for him to get the set if it's in Redwood Cove."

"I agree. That sounds like the best place to keep them. Let me give you the information you asked for."

He tore a piece of paper off a notepad and jotted down his phone and fax numbers. We joined the others and told them what we had decided. The open case and the daggers were at the end of the dining room table.

"I'd like to take photos to send to Michael Corrigan when I get back to town so we can get the process rolling as quickly as possible."

The others nodded their understanding, and I took several pictures with my cell phone. Rudy then closed the case, wrapped it in the protective cover, and placed it in his battered briefcase.

Timur stood and put his hand on Rudy's arm. "It's been such a pleasure to be in your company again. As you said, this is the family home. Verushka, Clay, and I have talked, and we'd like you to come live with us." He turned to Ivan. "You, too, of course, Ivan."

Clay gave a rueful laugh. "As I said earlier, we have plenty of rooms. They are part of the upkeep challenge."

"You don't need to decide now," Timur said. "Think about it."

"I shall," Rudy replied. "The home is magnificent and brings back many wonderful memories of the good times in Russia. I, too, have enjoyed being together again."

The brothers loaded the trunk with their newly acquired inheritance into my Jeep. We said our good-byes with promises to get together again. Then Rudy, Ivan, and I, along with millions of dollars' worth of jeweled daggers, headed home. I kept glancing in my rearview mirror. I doubted anyone would be following us, but I was nervous about the cargo we had with us.

"Rudy," Ivan said, "I understand if you want to go live with Verushka and Timur. The place is your inheritance, not so much mine. They are your family."

Ivan had chosen the back seat. I glanced at him in the mirror and a sad, serious face reflected back at me.

Rudy turned around in the front seat and addressed his brother. "The grounds and furnishings are beautiful, but the sea is in my soul. And you… you are my brother. Our home is together near the sea."

Ivan's face broke into a smile. Rudy turned around to face forward.

Back at the mansion, I'd felt like Rudy had been tempted to take Timur up on his offer. I was relieved that wasn't the case.

We arrived at their home, and I went in with them, wanting to stay close until Rudy secured the valuable set. He departed immediately for the vault and returned about ten minutes later.

"Thank you for inviting me today. I had a lovely time…and we solved one of the mysteries." I looked at my watch. "I'm going to go watch the Cossacks practice, then I'll see you at the four o'clock meeting."

"The group will be thrilled to hear about the dagger being sorted out," Rudy said. "May Ivan and I go with you to the festival field? I received a message on my phone about an impromptu committee meeting being arranged because a number of the performers are still onsite."

"Of course. Then I can take you on to the Silver Sentinels' meeting."

We all piled into the Jeep once again. The parking area was almost deserted. I found a space in the first row, with the entry road in front of me. I could see a number of different groups practicing in the field.

"Where are you meeting?" I asked.

"Bellington Bed and Breakfast," Rudy replied. "A number of committee members are staying there."

Maude's place. "I know where it is." I checked the time. "I'm going to watch the Cossacks for about an hour. I'd like to get back to the inn a bit before the meeting so I can update the charts. If you get done before I return, you could wait for me out front and watch the performers."

"Good idea," Ivan said.

"If you're not there, I'll come to get you. What room are you in?"

"Room six on the second floor. There are steps at the back of the building," Rudy said.

"Okay. I'm going to text Corrigan before I go. See you in a bit."

The brothers got out and headed for the B and B. I sent a short message to Corrigan, with a promise of more details to come, and attached the photos I had taken.

I reached behind the car seat and pulled out my cowboy boots. I exchanged the flats I'd worn for the tea for footwear more appropriate for the grassy field. I surveyed the area and spotted the Cossacks in the distance, near where they'd been yesterday.

I started to get out of the Jeep but stopped when my phone alerted me to a text. Corrigan responded that he'd love to help with the dagger set and wanted me to send him contact information so his lawyer could fax forms. More importantly, he wanted to arrange for a security firm to pick up the set tomorrow. He needed to know, as soon as possible, when the brothers would be available.

Getting the daggers squared away warranted interrupting the meeting. I got out, locked the Jeep, and headed for the Bellington inn.

I spotted Maude on the front porch. A dancing group performed a short distance away from her in the field, and she was clapping enthusiastically along with the music. I didn't stop to talk as I made my way through the parking area at the side of the building to get to the back entrance.

As I passed a white van, I saw the word *ouch* on a dent and realized it was the same one I'd seen parked at the marina. I froze. The vehicle had been there during the time Rick was murdered. It didn't necessarily mean there was a connection, but that was for Stanton to figure out.

I took a quick picture of the dent, and one of the license plate, and texted it to Stanton with a short message. Then I followed the garden fence around to the back and found a gate. I climbed the stairs and opened the back door. A narrow hallway with four doors greeted me. Number six was the second one on the left, and I heard voices. I raised my arm to knock.

A hand clamped over my mouth.

A muscular arm wrapped around my waist.

Chapter 27

I rammed my elbows back and into the person's sides and kicked a shin.

"Knock it off," a masculine voice growled.

I kept hitting and kicking.

He lifted me off the ground and banged on the door a couple of times with his foot. "Let me in."

The door opened, and he dragged me inside. I quit struggling when I saw Rudy and Ivan sitting in chairs with their arms tied behind their backs. The two crewmembers I'd seen at the trailer stood behind them with guns in their hands.

Alena held a gun to Ivan's head but spoke to me. "So nice of you to join us. You've done me a great favor by dropping in." She looked at the man holding me. "Let her go."

He released me, and he took his hand away from my mouth. I shot a quick glance at my assailant and saw a tall bulky man with a long bushy beard who I hadn't seen before. Alena swung the gun in my direction and looked at Rudy. "Now, you will take me to where you have the gold coins or your friend will die."

Rudy nodded. "I will show you. Don't hurt Kelly."

Alena addressed the men standing behind the brothers. "Take them to the van. I'll join you in a few minutes."

Rudy looked at me. "I'm so sorry you got involved in this, Kelly."

"Rudy—"

"Shut up," Alena said to me, and jabbed Ivan with the gun for emphasis.

I didn't try to speak again.

The crewmembers, who I now knew were henchmen, escorted Rudy and Ivan out.

Alena smirked. "Yes, you've helped me immensely." She turned to the one who had grabbed me. "Tie her up. We'll keep her alive for now, in case I need her for leverage. I'll let you know when we have the gold. Tonight, come back, take her to the woods, and shoot her."

My stomach flipped over. Apparently, she'd learned more than cooking from her father.

Alena kept the gun trained on me. "I don't have any more rope with me. Use the plastic strings from the blinds."

The man took a knife from his pocket and cut several pieces of string. He tied my hands behind my back. "Get down on the floor on your stomach."

I did, and he bound my feet. Then he took another piece of cord, bent my legs, and tied my hands to my feet.

Hog-tied.

For extra measure, he tied a cord from my arms to a sturdy-looking table under a window. "Wouldn't want you to wiggle across the room, now would we?"

As he finished tying me up, Alena went to the bed and took one of the pillowcases. She tossed it at him. "Use this for a gag."

He did as instructed.

"We'll leave for San Francisco as soon as we have the money and dispose of the brothers on the way. I will expect you back tomorrow morning," she said to him.

She left without another look in my direction. The man tested my ties, seemed satisfied, and followed her out, closing and locking the door behind him.

I began to struggle. The plastic cord gave a little. I strained to push my feet apart and gained a couple of inches. I rubbed my right foot against my left, working to push off my boot. After a couple of tries, I succeeded. With my foot now free, I was able to work off the right boot in a matter of minutes. I was thankful I'd chosen to go for the larger size when I bought them.

Fortunately, he hadn't tied me real close to the table. His goal was for it to be an anchor to keep me from moving around the room. I rolled over to it. He'd knotted the cord behind one of the legs, and I couldn't reach it with my fingers, because my hands were so closely bound.

Now what?

A lamp with a base that looked like a wood burl was in the center of the table. If there was some way for me to kick the lamp out the window, Maude would hear it. I tried to stand, but the cord to the table was too short.

However, I could sit up. I remembered a yoga move I'd learned called a shoulder stand. I turned my back to the table, put my hands into the small of my back, and pushed my legs straight up. I tilted them back and aimed for the lamp on the table. I bent my knees and, with all the force I could muster, thrust them against the lamp.

I never thought the sound of breaking glass would be so welcome.

A few minutes later, I heard a pounding on the door.

"What's going on in there?" Maude shouted. "You open this door right now, or I will."

After a short pause, I heard the rattle of the lock, the doorknob turn, and Maude stormed in.

She stopped in her tracks when she saw me. "Kelly! Oh my gosh."

Maude ran to me, dropped to her knees, and untied the pillowcase.

"Maude, they've got Ivan and Rudy Doblinsky. They're going to kill them."

Maude tried to untie my hands to no avail. She pulled a pair of small gardening clippers from her pocket. "Who are you talking about?"

"Alena Stepanova and some of the festival crewmembers. You need to call the police. They're headed for the Doblinsky brothers' house."

The cords dropped off my hands.

I grabbed my boots, put them on, and stood. "Every minute counts. I'm going to go see what I can do."

"Got it." She pulled out a cell phone from another pocket on her apron.

I ran out the doorway and down the hall. I clambered down the steps, around the back of the yard, and sprinted toward the road. Once there, I ran as fast as I could toward where I'd parked the Jeep.

I heard the sound of pounding hooves approaching.

Yaro appeared beside me in the field, reining his horse in to keep up with me. Worry filled his face. "Kelly, I saw you running. Is everything all right? Do you need help?"

"Friends…trouble…" I panted. "Need to…get to car."

"I will take you," he said and stopped his horse.

He took his right foot out of the stirrup and reached out to me with his hand. I took it, placed my right foot in the stirrup, and he pulled me up. I swung my left leg over the back of the horse and grabbed Yaro around the waist. The horse leaped into a gallop. We raced toward the parking lot.

"Green Jeep, front row!" I yelled in his ear.

He nodded.

I realized the noise of pounding hooves had increased. Yaro's friends had joined us. The Cossacks and I thundered down the field. Wind whistled in my ears. It was a jarring ride on the rump of the horse, and I held on tightly.

My Jeep was easy to spot, and Yaro headed straight for it. He stopped his horse next to the driver's door. The other riders had pulled up as well, their horses snorting and pawing the ground. I held on to the back of the saddle, took my left foot out of the stirrup, swung my leg over the back of the horse, and slipped my right foot out. I let go and slid to the ground.

"Thank you—" As I turned to my car, I saw the man who had tied me up. He saw me at the same time, reached in his pocket, and pulled out a phone. I knew if he alerted the others I was loose, they might shoot Ivan and Rudy.

I looked at the Cossacks and yelled, "Stop him from making a call. They might kill my friends!"

The whip-wielding Cossack yelled, and his horse jumped forward and into a gallop. The rider's whip snaked out and coiled around the arm of Alena's henchman. He shrieked, and the phone flew out of his hand. The Cossack rode past the man, yanking him to the ground, then stopped.

The downed man tore the whip off his arm. As the henchman staggered to one knee, the lance-bearing rider pounded by him and whacked him on the back of the head. The man fell forward and was still. By that time, Yaro was there. He dismounted, pulled off his belt, and used it for a makeshift rope. He tied the man's hands behind his back. The other riders had formed a circle around the fallen man.

I didn't think they needed to worry that he'd be going anywhere soon. I heard a puttering noise and saw Maude arriving on a blue and white scooter.

"Kelly, go! I'll call the police again and tell them what's happened."

I didn't need another invitation. I jumped in my car, started it, and hit the gas. The wheels spun briefly, then I lurched forward onto the road and away from the horses and the men. I'd thank the Cossacks later.

I sped toward Ivan and Rudy's home, slowing as I neared it. I passed Alena's sports car a couple of blocks from the house. The police weren't there yet, and I saw the white van parked in their driveway.

I pulled in my vehicle crosswise behind the van, blocking it.

I could see the figure of a man in the driver's seat and a large passenger I suspected was Ivan. The man turned his head when I stopped my vehicle. I didn't recognize him. Alena had plenty of helpers.

I slid out of the Jeep, keeping low, and ran to the side of the house. There was a slope with a few bushes scattered around. I slid down a few feet and hunkered behind a bush. I knew they could find me if they searched, but I was counting on the police arriving and Alena's main concern being to escape.

I heard what I thought was Russian cursing from the driveway. Sirens sounded in the distance, and I began to work my way up the slope. I froze when I heard pounding feet above me. Glancing up, I saw Alena's driver running down the road. I peeked around the garage and saw Ivan alone in the van.

I ran to his door and opened it.

"Kelly, you here. Not hurt. Is good."

"Let's get you out of here."

Ivan's hands were tied, but not his legs. He turned and was about to scoot out when the front door opened. Alena emerged, holding a gun pointed at Rudy. Ivan returned to his original position. I ducked down out of sight, partially closing the vehicle's door. Her two coworkers followed, each carrying a chest I recognized as belonging to Rudy.

Two police cars arrived off to the right of the front yard and screeched to a halt. Officers emerged, guns drawn. Alena's lips set in a grim line.

"Do not try anything or he dies," she yelled. "We are going to drive away."

She walked Rudy toward the van. The sidewalk curved and met the van in the middle of its side. I inched up until I could look through the windows. Alena and her coworkers had their backs to the van.

A third police car arrived, and I recognized Stanton.

Alena's attention, and that of her cohorts, was focused on the police, watching for any move they might make. Ivan pushed open his door and slid out. He moved toward the front of the vehicle.

He suddenly ran at Alena.

"Alena, watch out!" the man next to her shouted as he glanced over his shoulder.

She twirled around and started to aim the gun at Ivan. Rudy jerked away. Alena moved her gun toward him. Ivan flung his large bulk against her. Alena went down, and he landed on top of her. The gun fell from her hand. One of the officers raced in and grabbed it.

"Get off me, you oaf!" she screamed.

"You plan to hurt me, my brother. I stay."

Stanton had the one with the shaved head in his sights. "Put down the chest slowly."

The man started to obey when the one with the tattoos dropped his chest and made a run for it. I turned and ran around to the back of the van. As he started to sprint past me, I stuck out my leg.

It hurt, but it felt good to see him fall on the ground.

"Gus, hold," I heard Stanton yell.

I saw the back of his police car was open. The bloodhound came bounding out and landed on top of the downed man with all four feet firmly planted.

"Call him off! Get him away from me!" the man screamed.

Gus wagged his tail.

The man seemed terrified of the dog. I suspected Gus just wanted to play. Gus leaned down his head, and I wondered if he was going to lick the man. A thread of drool began to detach itself from the bloodhound's jowls and make a slow journey downward. It came loose and landed on the man's forehead. He groaned, turned his head from side to side, and looked like he was going to be ill.

A fourth squad car arrived. It had come from a different direction, and I spied the runaway henchman in the back seat. A clean sweep.

An officer went to relieve Ivan of his immobilizing duties. Ivan rolled off Alena and stood. The policeman handcuffed her and walked her toward the cars.

Rudy went to his brother. I joined them, and Rudy and I worked on Ivan's tied hands. After much tugging, the rope came off, and he was free.

They hugged. No words were spoken.

Stanton had kept his gun pointed at the man with the shaved head and the henchman cooperated. The deputy sheriff had him turn around to be handcuffed. The bloodhound's catch was the last to be taken care of. The man was clearly shaken. Maybe he'd be willing to give some answers.

Stanton came to talk to me. "Quite the haul."

"I'm just glad it's over...Bill," I said.

"Me, too, Kelly."

Our unspoken acknowledgment the investigation was done.

I looked at my watch. Rudy, Ivan, and I still had time to make the Silver Sentinels' meeting. We had a lot to share.

Chapter 28

"I'll need to get a statement from the three of you," Deputy Stanton said.

We all nodded.

"Bill, we have a meeting at the inn," I said. "Could you come by and talk to us there? You could use the office."

"Sure. I'll accompany this crew to headquarters, then I'll text you when I'm on the way."

I smiled. "Great."

Stanton turned to Rudy. "Your coins are going to have to go into evidence. I'm sorry your secret will be out."

"Some of our secret," Rudy responded. "Not all of it."

"Will make statement money is in bank when it is returned," Ivan said.

I nodded in the direction the driver had run. "Bill, I saw Alena's car about two blocks away. It's a two-seater pearlescent sports car."

"Thanks, Kelly."

He walked off, and we all got in my Jeep and headed for Redwood Cove Bed and Breakfast. Rudy and Ivan were safe…and I had ridden with the Cossacks! We filled the others in on what had happened. Relief was evident on their faces as the realization that the unpleasant events surrounding Ivan and Rudy were at an end.

Bill texted and a short while later stopped by to take the statements. He promised to contact the Silver Sentinels when he had more to share and to wrap up loose ends. Mary, Gertie, and the Professor left, followed by Rudy and Ivan, after they talked with Deputy Stanton.

After taking my statement, he said. "Kelly, today would have had a different ending if you hadn't been able to think so fast and get away." He looked at his notes. "A shoulder stand. Really?"

"I've done a little yoga. It's a good thing that's one of the moves I learned."

"...and riding with the Cossacks. You never cease to amaze me."

I shared with him how the dagger had ended up on the boat, as well as the future of the knife set.

"There will be consequences for Clay," he said. "The family circumstances and his reason for what he did might help the judge be more lenient."

"He didn't harm anyone," I said.

"I know. But he sent us on a wild-goose chase that took a lot of police time." Stanton put his notepad away. "Lots to do. See you later."

After he left, I canceled Alena's personal room reservation for next weekend's Russian Heritage Committee.

She won't be needing it.

I kept the conference room reserved for the committee, figuring someone would contact me.

Toward the end of the week, Bill Stanton called, and I set up a meeting with the Silver Sentinels. Mary brought a new treat, strawberry cheesecake bars. We put up the charts, updated them, and got ready to add new information.

I heard a knock on the conference room door and opened it.

"Hi, Kelly." Bill held his Stetson in his hand.

"Come on in. We're all eager to hear what you have to share."

The officer settled himself at the table and looked at our notes hung around the room. "What would you like to know first?"

"Tell us about Alexander," Mary said. "What did you find out?"

Rudy stood and picked up a marker, prepared to write what Deputy Stanton had to say.

"Russian Treasures was a money laundering operation for a Russian crime syndicate. Turns out Alexander was using it for some illegal activities of his own, too. Thanks to your tip, Mary, we found stolen Russian antiques scattered throughout the store. After examining the ledgers, it appears he was skimming money from the coin trade as well."

The Professor twirled his pen. "Doesn't seem a smart move to steal from an organized crime group and use their store for his own purposes."

Stanton nodded. "Shortly after Alexander was killed, we received a call from an agent in San Francisco who works with undercover officers. News of Alexander's death and what he'd been up to had spread rapidly. Rumors made it clear he was executed."

"Why was he on the boat?" I asked.

"We're not positive, but we have a pretty good idea." Stanton looked at Rudy. "We found Alexander's appointment book, and it appears you planned in advance to meet with him to sell your coins."

"That's right. I didn't want to take a chance he'd be gone or too busy to talk with me," Rudy said.

Stanton took out his notepad from his pocket. "On those days, you and Ivan would leave the house in the morning and take the bus to the marina. After that, you'd get on the bus again and return to Redwood Cove and Alexander's shop."

Rudy looked startled. "How did you know?"

"We found reports in Alena's briefcase. She employed two men to follow both of you the days of two of your appointments. You had the same routine both times."

"Yes. We studied the bus schedule and found a good way to get to the *Nadia* and check on her, which we do once a week, and then get back to Redwood Cove."

"She had you followed the day before as well," Stanton said.

"What was she trying to find out?" I asked.

"We think she was working on figuring out the location of the gold coins," he replied. "Redwood Cove has no bank. The closest one is in Fort Peter. The brothers didn't go there the day before the meeting."

Gertie nodded. "So, she figured the money was at their house or on the *Nadia*."

"That's what we think," Stanton said. "It was an educated guess on her part. We suspect she, and possibly some of her men, met Alexander at the boat and searched it. After coming up empty-handed, she disposed of Alexander. She didn't need him anymore, and she had a message to send."

"Quite the cold-blooded woman," Mary said. "Can you prove she killed him?"

"We can prove her gun was used. A clever lawyer can claim one of her men used it to murder Alexander."

"What about Rick?" Gertie asked.

"I doubt he knew organized crime was involved. We think Alena and her men followed him to the boat and surprised him, and he tried to defend himself. We found a gun in his hand."

"Why didn't they try to hide his body to delay people finding it?" I asked.

"They did," Stanton responded. "We found his blood on a tarp. They probably covered him and then searched the boat. They came up empty-handed. The only reason our people found the coin was because they used a metal detector." Stanton looked at the charts. "I see you thought the body might have been left there to implicate Ivan."

The Professor put down his pen. "Yes, because of the fight."

"I would agree," Stanton said. "Rick's murder became one more case for us to deal with, and the altercation between Rick and Ivan provided an opportunity to possibly throw us off track."

"For all she knew, we could almost be out of money," Rudy said. "Why take the risk of getting caught?"

"It was a gamble, but she did her homework there as well." Stanton stood, went over to the coffee area, and poured himself a cup. "One of Alena's employees hacked into Goldstein's computer, and she tracked some of Harvey's gold sales. People who buy those coins form a limited market. She found out Harvey had been selling them for a long time. She wasn't able to tell if they belonged to you two or Clay, but her notes showed Clay's last two sales to Alexander were coins of a much lesser value. You were her best bet."

He went on to tell us she'd discovered their connection to an aristocratic family, and he'd found notes about the brothers' background. Alena had seen the Facebook information about the dagger and had added that to her files.

"She certainly was thorough," Gertie said. "Too bad she didn't put her brain to good use."

"I agree," Stanton said. "Are there any other loose ends?"

We scanned the charts. All the answers were there.

"Thank you, Bill. It feels good to have everything tied up," I said.

I shuddered a bit when I said *tied up*, thinking about the experience I'd had.

Stanton stood and put on his hat. "You're welcome."

He left, and the meeting took on a jovial tone as we chatted and took down the charts. I said I'd keep them until the case was closed, in case they proved helpful in some way. It was Thursday, and we made plans to meet on Sunday to decide which community project we might want to get involved in.

I returned to my rooms, went to my computer, and checked messages. One, from Corrigan, said an international bidding war had started for the daggers and their case. He was enjoying handling the offers and said the family members would be well taken care of when the set sold.

Vladimir emailed, saying he'd be in charge of the Russian Heritage Committee meeting planned for this coming Saturday. He asked if he could meet with me and the Silver Sentinels. I wrote back to tell him he was welcome to join us on Sunday at one o'clock. I wondered why he wanted to see us but didn't ask. I'd know soon enough.

The next two days passed quickly. Helen again baked baklava for Saturday's group. I wasn't quite as afraid of the fragile dough as I had been before, but I still kept my distance. Sunday arrived, and the group gathered in the conference room. We carried out the usual routine. Helen and I put out drinks, Mary arrived with treats, and the sound of Ivan's voice boomed down the hallway as the brothers arrived. It was a routine I loved.

Vladimir appeared in the doorway at the appointed time.

"Come in," I said. "Please join us. Refreshments are on the sideboard. Help yourself and take a seat."

"Thank you," he said. "I just had lunch, so I'll pass on the food and drink."

"What can we do for you?" the Professor asked.

Vladimir remained standing. "I've learned a lot about your group in the past week. I want to thank you all for what you did to solve the murders of the two men, Alexander and Rick, and the help you gave to two of our Russian Heritage Committee members, Ivan and Rudy."

"They are two of our own and dear friends," Mary said. "We are there for each other."

"So I've heard," Vladimir said. "Your community is very fortunate to have such a group as yourselves." He pulled an envelope from his jacket pocket. "I have a present for you as a way of saying thanks."

Vladimir opened the envelope and put what looked like a stack of tickets on the table. I reached over and took one. The rectangular cardstock had an elaborate design of red roses and gold filigree around the sides. The center read *Russian Heritage Formal Ball*, and the price of $175 under it.

"These are tickets for you to attend a dance we are putting on," Vladimir said. "There are enough for all of you, as well as a number of your friends."

Talk of attending a formal ball is back.

I recalled the thoughts I'd had when Alena mentioned it, and how much I'd be out of my element. I'd pass on this event.

Vladimir stood between Ivan and Rudy. He rested his right hand on Rudy's shoulder and his left on Ivan's. "I have talked with Rudy and Ivan. We plan to honor their family. The Russian community now knows the story. It will be a celebration of their being reunited."

Rudy nodded. "Please say you will all come. This means a lot to Ivan and me."

Ivan nodded. "Have been talking with Timur and Verushka. Becoming like family. They will be there along with Clay."

"I will wear my father's uniform." His eyes teared a bit. "Please say you'll come."

It sounds like I'm on my way to a formal Russian ball after all.

Chapter 29

"But…but…" spluttered Gertie. "Me? In a ball gown?"

I knew how she felt.

"You will be beautiful," Vladimir said. "I must go now. I have another appointment."

"Thank you for the tickets," I said. *I think.*

The others all added their thanks. Vladimir said good-bye and went on his way.

Rudy passed out the tickets and gave me what was left. "Please give these to your friends."

"We have more to say," Ivan said.

Rudy nodded. "Yes, Ivan and I talked and want to pay for the gowns for the ladies and a tux for you, Professor."

"Oh, no," Mary said. "I can't let you do that."

"Same here," Gertie chimed in.

I wasn't to be left out. "Thank you, Rudy, but that doesn't feel right."

"I'm with the ladies on this," the Professor said.

Rudy straightened his shoulders and gave us a stern look. "You all give generously of your time and your caring. It's your nature. Accepting a gift is a form of giving."

"Give us opportunity to thank you," Ivan said.

"Our hearts are filled with gratitude toward all of you," Rudy said. "Sometimes it is important to let people give to you."

Mary gave a slight smile. "That was lovely. I accept."

Gertie sighed. "What would my Pennsylvania Dutch grandmother say about buying a formal gown?"

Rudy reached across the table and patted her hand. "She would say *do it for your friends.*"

"She probably would," Gertie said. "Thank you, Rudy and Ivan."

The Professor and I once again followed along, agreeing to accept their offer.

Ivan reached for one of the dessert bars Mary had brought. "Good. Is settled."

"Besides," Rudy said, "the dagger set will be bringing in more money than Ivan and I can imagine."

"You all should know I can't dance," I said. "Please don't give me a bad time for just standing at the ball."

"I will be delighted to teach you," the Professor said. "We have plenty of time before the event. It's not for three months."

He didn't know I had two left feet.

"Well…we can give it a try."

"Nonsense. There's nothing to it," he commented. "It'll be fun."

I thought of Scott and the pie incident. The Professor didn't know what he was getting into, but he would soon enough. I hoped he had sturdy shoes.

Gertie and Mary made plans to meet the next afternoon to start shopping online. The Professor offered to drive Rudy and Ivan to the largest nearby town inland that was big enough to rent and sell tuxedos. They'd make a day of it, with lunch at a famous Italian restaurant. I went to call my sister. I needed her help with the formal gown business.

I settled on the window seat in my quarters and dialed. Her familiar voice answered.

"Hi, Sis. How are the kids?" I asked.

"Doing great. They're down for a nap right now. What are you up to?"

"Learning more about the town and the inn."

I'd tell her about the festival and Rudy and Ivan's relatives another time. I never shared what I did with the Silver Sentinels in the crime-solving arena so as not to worry them.

"So…I've been invited to a formal Russian ball."

"What!" she shrieked in my ear. "You mean like in wearing a formal gown? Long gloves? High heels?"

"Yes, all those things."

"Oh." The short word was a long sigh filled with fantasies of a formal ball followed by a pause. "How exciting!" she shrieked again.

"Not so much for me. Sis, you were a perfect girly girl growing up. I was the spitting image of a tomboy."

"You'll have fun."

"I grew up watching *Lassie* and *Rin Tin Tin* while you watched and rewatched *Cinderella* and *Snow White*."

"You'll look so beautiful."

"I was practicing barrel racing for the next rodeo while you learned to embroider."

"Wait until you start shopping for gowns! You'll have a great time doing that."

"That's what I called you about. That and to say hi. Will you help me find a dress?"

"Will I help you find a dress? Are you kidding? Of course!"

We decided she'd send me photos of her top online picks. After I chose the one I wanted, it would be shipped to the ranch. She insisted on everything fitting perfectly for the family and always made any necessary alterations. She had all my measurements. I gave her the date of the dance. I could tell she could hardly wait to get off the phone and start shopping.

In the following week, I had my first dance lesson with the Professor. Originally, he had said we'd practice once a week. After our first encounter, he changed it to three times a week.

I gave the remaining tickets to Daniel, Helen, Bill, and Scott. They were thrilled. Corrigan sold the dagger set for untold millions to a museum and offered to set up a trust fund for Timur, Verushka, and Clay. They would be set financially for the rest of their lives.

During a conversation with him, I mentioned the Russian ball. He told me to save him a dance and he would be there. He promised to arrange for transportation for the Silver Sentinels and me that evening.

My sister sent me a dozen photos. As I looked at them one by one, I found they were all lovely but didn't spark the excitement my sister exuded when she found a piece of clothing she loved.

Then I got to the last picture. I gasped. This was the one. Simple. Elegant. Gorgeous. Emerald green silk cascaded to the floor with a V-neck bodice. The back had a V as well, but deeper. I emailed her my choice, and she immediately replied it was the one she hoped I would pick.

A month later, the box with the dress arrived. My sister had made fast work of the alterations. I took it to my quarters, opened the box, and folded back the tissue paper covering it. A beam of sunlight hit the emerald green silk, and it seemed to shimmer in response. Carefully, I lifted it out of the box and laid it out on the bed. The gown was even more beautiful than I had expected.

I touched it and marveled at its softness. My ex and I had had a simple wedding with no wedding gown involved. I wore a nice dress, and he was in a suit. I'd never worn anything like this.

Two tissue-wrapped packages were in the bottom of the box. I picked one up and put it on the bed next to the dress. I opened the paper and found long black satin gloves, a small beaded handbag, and a jewel-studded hair clip, along with a note.

Here are a few additional items to make your evening even more magical.

My amazing sister. The last package revealed a pair of black satin high heels and another note.

I thought you might not think about the heels until the last minute, so here they are.

She was so right. They only footwear I'd brought with me that had any kind of heel were my cowboy boots.

I put on the dress and felt transformed, as if I was part of a fairy tale. I twisted up my hair and fastened it with the sparkling clip. That and the gloves took the experience to another level. I slipped into the heels and realized I had a lot of practicing ahead. It had been a long time since I'd worn high heels, much less danced in them.

I was excited. I had to admit it. My sister had altered the gown, and it was a perfect fit. Once I learned to walk and dance in the shoes, I'd be ready.

Rudy called the next day and asked if he and Ivan could come over for a few minutes. I told him that would be fine. I'd be in all day, doing an inventory of our pantry. When they arrived, we went into the conference room. Rudy had brought his briefcase. We all sat and Rudy put the case down, opened it, and pulled out a box.

"Ivan and I have a present for you. We wouldn't be alive if it wasn't for you."

"Wait," I said. "You've done enough with offering to buy the ball gown."

Ivan rested his hand on my arm. "Is something special from us."

Rudy opened the box, and I saw the necklace Ivan had shown us in the vault, the one that had belonged to their mother. "Our mother would want you to have this. You saved her sons."

"We look at sometimes and remember her," Ivan said. "We can look at it on you and do the same."

I was close to speechless. The diamonds sparkled and glittered in the overhead light. "But…what about family members you could give it to? Like Verushka and Clay's sister."

"We are giving it to family…you. You are family to us." Rudy took it out of the box. He unclasped it and held it out to me. "May I put it on you?"

I blinked rapidly to hold back the tears that were forming. "Yes, Rudy. I'd be flattered to have you do that."

I turned and held up my hair. Rudy put the necklace over my head and then around my throat and closed the clasp. I stood and went to a mirror at the end of the conference room. I'd never worn anything like this in my life. I touched the necklace and thought of their mother, Tatiana, and all she'd been through.

"Please accept," Ivan said.

"It would mean much to us for it to go to someone we care about," Rudy said.

I took a deep breath. "Thank you for this precious gift. I will always think of you, your mother, and the prince when I wear it."

We hugged each other, and some tears found their way down my cheeks. Ivan gave me the box, and they left. I looked again at myself in the mirror. The diamonds seemed to wink at me as if to say, *We're the finishing touch.*

The day of the ball arrived. Michael planned to pick up Gertie and Mary and then come for me. One of the veterans from the Community Center would use the company Mercedes and get Rudy, Ivan, and the Professor. Daniel had made arrangements for one of his employees at Ridley House to come over to tend to our guests and be with Allie and Tommy. The kids would look after the dogs.

I prepared an early light meal and began to get ready. My sister had sent me eye shadow she thought would go well with my gown. I did my makeup routine, then coiled up my hair onto the top of my head, reminiscent of Audrey Hepburn in *Breakfast at Tiffany's*. That completed, I slipped into the dress and put on the necklace, along with simple stud diamond earrings. I wore my daily gold bracelet, which felt like a trusted friend, one I needed tonight…especially when I looked at the stranger in the mirror.

I was back into the fairy tale again, only this time I wore the gift of a prince to the woman he loved. I went to join the others in the main room.

Michael Corrigan and Bill Stanton stood next to the granite counter, talking. The two tall muscular men made a striking sight in their tuxedos. Gertie wore a silver gown with a cape covering her shoulders. Pink ruffles and lace suited Mary.

Gus sprawled on the extra bed we kept for guest canines. His long lanky frame covered it from one end to the other, and his ears dangled over the side. Princess had a coat to match Mary's pink gown and sported a white leather collar dotted with pink rhinestones. I watched as the tan Chihuahua trotted over and claimed Fred's bed. The basset hound, sitting next to Tommy, who was in the beanbag chair, looked perplexed.

Tommy jumped up. "I'll go get her bed." He dashed out of the room.

Michael came over to me. “You look fabulous, Kelly.”

He glanced at the necklace but didn’t ask anything. I’d tell him about it later.

“Thank you, Michael. You make quite the handsome sight yourself in your formal attire.”

The back door opened, and Helen entered the room. She looked stunning in a ruby red gown that accented the pink glow in her cheeks. I remembered when I first saw her looking pale and gaunt after losing her husband and moving to Redwood Cove. In the beginning, it hadn’t been the place she’d dreamed of to help Tommy cope. Times had changed. Deputy Stanton—Bill—stood next to her.

Tommy came running into the room and skidded to a stop and dropped the dog bed. His eyes widened at the sight of his mother. “M…M…Mom?”

Helen went to him and gave him a hug. “Remember to brush your teeth before you go to bed.”

She was definitely still his mom.

Allie and Daniel arrived. He provided another handsome addition to our male population. Allie picked up the little dog bed and put it next to Fred’s bed. She picked up Princess and placed her on it, and Fred immediately claimed his cushion.

We all went around complimenting each other. There were lots of oohs and ahhs. Michael said it was time to go, and we headed for the door.

Helen said, “We’ll join you as soon as Sadie from the Ridley House gets here. She texted she’s on her way.”

Off we went to the Russian formal ball. The veterans were the valets for the evening. Committee members checked us in and gave dance cards to Gertie, Mary, and me. I felt someone beside me and turned to find Scott next to me.

“You look beautiful,” he said. “But you always do, whether in jeans or a ball gown.”

He couldn’t look more striking himself.

“Thank you.”

“I want the first dance and the last dance and a few in between,” he said.

I handed him my card, and he wrote in his name. We walked into the ballroom. Enormous vases of multicolored flowers decorated tables where dancers could sit and rest during the evening. Their scent perfumed the air. The orchestra played a few notes.

The first dance had started.

Scott took me in his arms and the music began.

About the Author

Janet Finsilver and her husband live in the San Francisco Bay Area. She loves animals and has two dogs—Kylie and Ellie. Janet enjoys horseback riding, snow skiing, and cooking. She is currently working on her next Redwood Cove mystery. Readers can visit her website at www.JanetFinsilver.com.

CPSIA information can be obtained
at www.ICGtesting.com
Printed in the USA
LVHW111416080419
613369LV00001B/148/P